103RD MERIDIAN

a novel by

TOM CLAFFEY

TREATY OAK PUBLISHERS

PUBLISHER'S NOTE

The New Mexico Commission of Public Records has granted permission to reprint the following archived documents:

From the Gov. William McDonald Papers, Collection No. 1959-094, Box SN 17249, folder 521, New Mexico State Archives.

"Texas, New Mexico, and Oklahoma Boundary Lines, Letter from the Secretary of the Interior transmitting the Report of the Astronomical Investigations of the Texas, New Mexico, and Oklahoma Boundary Line, Dec. 19, 1905. Document No. 259, House of Representatives, 59th Congress, First Session"

From the Gov. William McDonald Papers, Collection No. 1959-094, Box SN 17249, folder 421, New Mexico State Archives.

"Three-page letter, dated March 12, 1906, from U.S. Department on the Interior to H. J. Hagerman"

Printed and published in the United States of America

TREATY OAK PUBLISHERS
ISBN-13: 978-1-943658-05-3
ISBN-10: 1-943658-05-6

ALSO BY TOM CLAFFEY

Acknowledgments

Very special thanks to:

Frankie Aragon, County Assessor, Union County, New Mexico
Victoria Baker, Executive Director, Herzstein Memorial Museum, Clayton, New Mexico
Roy Chavez, Union County General Hospital, Clayton, New Mexico
Craig Colter, Colonel, USAF, Retired, Albuquerque, New Mexico
James A. Grant, M.D., F.A.C.S. - Santa Fe, New Mexico; San Diego, California
Larry Haight, Sierra Aviation, Santa Fe, New Mexico
David Keyea, rancher and writer, Clayton, New Mexico
Terry L. Martin, Publisher, Union County Leader, Clayton, New Mexico
J.D. Miera, Foreman, Ringbone Cattle Company, Glenville, New Mexico
Sibel Melik, State Records Center and Archives, Santa Fe, New Mexico
Steve Reiter, U.S. Geological Survey, Denver, Colorado
Jon Rose, City Manager, Texline, Texas
Robert A. Rubenstein, M.D., La Mesa, California
Lee Scholes, rancher, horseman, commercial pilot, Magdalena, New Mexico
Summer Short, EMS Captain, Clayton Fire and Rescue, Clayton, New Mexico
Edward Sisneros and Michael DeHerrera, Clayton Municipal Airport, Clayton, New Mexico
Judy Steen, Executive Director, Clayton-Union County Chamber of Commerce
Bill Tefft, New Mexico Public Lands Information Center, Santa Fe, New Mexico
Arnold Vigil, Senior Archivist, State of New Mexico
Summer Wood, University of New Mexico Taos Summer Writers' Conference

My deepest gratitude to Cynthia Stone, a dear and special lady, for her editorial guidance – and her friendship.

To
Laura Brodie

a novel by

TOM CLAFFEY

CHAPTER 1

ordon Meese sat facing the door of the Rabbit Ear Café in Clayton, New Mexico, during a summer lunch hour in 2014.

He was enjoying a ham and cheese sandwich. It had been several months since he'd occupied a barber's chair. The collar of his khaki work shirt, hidden by thick gray hair, was barely visible. Beside his plate was a geological report about the dinosaur footprints at nearby Clayton Lake—nearly 800 prints found since 1982. Cheese dripped from between the slices of bread onto the oval plate. He reached in a shirt pocket for his ever-present spiral pad and made a note about the prints.

Concentrating on the dinosaur report, Gordon ignored the steady traffic on South 1st Street as well as customers entering or leaving the café. The only sounds in the restaurant were the murmured conversations of other customers and chatter from the kitchen.

The smell of burgers and green chili drifted across the room, and Gordon inhaled deeply, held it for a few seconds, then returned his attention to the report. He felt comfortable in the pinewood-walled dining room, at his usual table near the four large windows. Behind him, art objects and black metal wall sculptures adorned the walls: *Harley Davidson Motorcycles; Live, Laugh, Love; Texas Tech;* silhouette of a cowboy kneeling beside his horse in prayer.

Gordon pushed the dinosaur report to the side and pulled an aeronautical chart of the state of New Mexico from a manila folder.

Sarah Jane, his favorite waitress, paused at his table to refill his coffee mug. "Thought you'd be up buzzing around, exploring the great outdoors in your Skyhawk today."

Without taking his eyes from the chart, Gordon grunted.

"Whatcha reading? More of that New Mexico/Texas border thing you seem to be so hung-up on?"

He tapped his finger on a spot on the chart. "Sarah Jane, I'm determined to get to the bottom of this."

She gaped at him, her mouth twisted in a wry grin. "Do the folks at the State Land Office know what you're up to?"

"What business is it of theirs? I don't work for them anymore. I retired. Remember?" He grunted again. "I work for me."

"I just think you are too obsessed with an imaginary boundary error. It's like you want to start a border war with Texas!" Sarah Jane chuckled as she strolled to the next table, the coffee pot just missing the head of an unsuspecting customer.

"The border," Gordon growled, "should be the 103rd meridian—not almost three miles to its west, goddamnit!"

"Yep," Sarah Jane shot back over her shoulder. "And that thing's got you right around your neck, Mr. Meese!"

"Humph!" He grunted again. "You don't know what you're talking about, young lady."

As Gordon glanced up at the slightly off-center wall clock over the door, a woman entered the restaurant by herself. A touch of class about her, mid-to-late-thirties, dark brown hair. She made eye contact with no one as she walked to a small table to the right front of his.

He lifted the ham and cheese and checked her out over the top of his steel-rimmed glasses. She wore a burgundy colored broomstick skirt and a white blouse.

With her eyes downcast, the woman read the menu and tucked her left leg beneath her on the chair, leaving only her right foot touching the brown concrete floor. On the right side of her neck was a dime-sized pink birthmark. She glanced at him for an instant, then returned to the menu.

Gordon stared at the tabletop without seeing it. The woman reminded him of Molly, the beautiful girl from Oak Grove, Kentucky, who had put off plans to become a schoolteacher to marry him instead. His mind raced through the twenty-five years of frequent overseas deployments that allowed little time for home or family. And later, when he shed his uniform to seek rewards in civilian life, there came frustration and dissatisfaction with job offers. Followed by a suspended job search and more time spent at home with his new friend, Jack Daniels. Black Label.

Molly, how could you leave? How could I have let… He shook his head as if awakening from heavy sleep, then took another bite from the sandwich and set it back on the plate.

The woman gave her lunch order to Sarah Jane. When Sarah Jane left, she looked down at the pages of the local weekly newspaper, appearing to read them. She turned her head to a soft *beep, beep*. Gordon watched her retrieve her cell phone from a brown leather purse and stare at the small phone screen for several moments. Then she returned to the newspaper until her lunch was served.

Again, *beep, beep*. She glanced at the screen and her eyes welled. After several moments she wiped away a tear, returned the phone to her purse, and pulled a white handkerchief from a skirt pocket—the way Molly would have done. She lowered her gaze and brooded at the damp crumpled handkerchief in her hands.

Gordon continued stealing glances. He wished he were seated closer to her.

Two ranchers entered the café and stopped in front of his table, blocking his view.

"Damn, Gordon, when you concentrate, you really concentrate," the younger rancher said. He wore a chocolate brown Stetson with a narrow dust-covered sweat ring.

Gordon looked up. Ty Daggett and his friend Henry Lewis owned adjoining ranches southeast of town.

Henry, in his mid-sixties, stroked his bushy gray moustache. "How you getting along, Gordon? Enjoying retirement?"

Gordon reached out and shook their hands. "Got no complaints." He smiled. "What brings you fellas to town?"

"Doing a little horse trading." Henry grinned.

"Horse buying is more like it," Ty said. He was nearly thirty years younger than his neighbor. "Henry has a sorrel colt I'm interested in."

"Sounds like heavy negotiating." Gordon tapped the nosepiece of his glasses.

"Gordon," Ty said, "I hear you're looking into the border dispute between New Mexico and Texas. Found anything yet?"

Gordon shook his head. "Not yet. Ken Lively and I are trying to locate a few survey markers and monuments. And I'm visiting the State Archives Office in Santa Fe tomorrow."

"Keep us posted," Ty said. "Henry's land butts up against the present state line and a portion of the Daggett Ranch extends into Texas."

"I'll let you know what I find." The men shook hands. Henry and Ty walked to a table beside one of the windows.

Gordon finished his lunch and glanced again at the dark-haired woman. He watched her looking down at her clasped hands, watched tears return once more, and yearned to reach across the space between their tables. Instead, he eased his plate to the side, glanced at his wristwatch, put on his jacket, and left.

HE CLIMBED INTO his 1969 Willys Jeep and drove out of the restaurant parking lot. Tempted as he was to turn around, Gordon continued down 1st Street to Main Street. He headed northeast on Main, hoping the woman might somehow know there was another soul in this world who cared—someone who saw she was in a world of hurt, who yearned to help.

Eight miles ahead on US Highway 56 were two boundary markers Gordon needed to find. He glanced at the dime store clock taped to the Jeep's instrument panel and shoved his boot against the accelerator. He was running late. In the topless, doorless vehicle, his loose gray hair became a feathered frenzy. He ran his bony hand through it as a tumbleweed shot in from the right and wedged itself between the steering wheel and the dashboard.

"Holy shit!" Gordon grabbed the root base of the weed and threw it over his shoulder into the bullying wind.

KENNETH LIVELY, A LOCAL surveyor from across the state line in Texline, Texas, stood scanning the fertile grasslands and cornfields near the intersection of Highway 56 and Rinker Road. He imagined the undulating hills of New Mexico, Oklahoma, and Texas, under water when they formed the bed of an ancient seaway.

Visibility worsened in the wind and blowing dust. He bent down and read a ground level concrete marker at his feet: U.S. Department of the Interior, Bureau of Land Management, Cadastral Survey, 1991.

"This is it." He smiled and scratched his chin, eager to share the discovery with Gordon.

Ken stood and looked toward the west at the landmark Rabbit Ears Mountain, seven miles northwest of Clayton. Named for the Comanche Chief Rabbit

Ears, he had read of it being a welcome sight to those hardy souls traveling the 800 miles from Independence, Missouri, to Santa Fe. He tried to picture 80 wagons making it through extreme weather, waist-deep rivers, and encounters with Plains Indian each year, wondering if he would have died of hunger and thirst, as many of them did.

A sudden horrific gust of wind interrupted his day-dreaming and lifted the worn western hat from his head, sending it rolling fifty yards down the dirt Rinker Road. He chased after it until he caught it, then returned to the survey marker. He glanced at his wristwatch then, looked southward, hoping to see Gordon's Jeep.

CHAPTER 2

The hand Ken now placed on the bronze U.S. Department of the Interior plate still bore the burn scars from that day during Operation Desert Storm in 1991, where he first knew Gordon Meese

He glanced at his wristwatch again. Strong winds from the east with gusts powerful enough to bend tall corn stalks to the ground, forced him into a wide stance in his heavy work boots. He pressed his hat against his head as a wheelbarrow-sized tumbleweed barreled down Rinker Road, barely missing his Ford F150 pickup before slamming into a barbed wire fence.

Kenneth squinted as he stared across the fields into the distance. The land could have been Hafar Al-Batin in northeastern Saudi Arabia, where their unit had come under heavy bombardment from Saddam Hussein's Iraqi troops. The mountains grew hazy, then disappeared, and then the dense air from the Middle East grazed his cheeks.

BUCK SERGEANT KENNETH LIVELY sat in the right seat of the M1151 Humvee "gun truck," with his crew:

the driver, a corporal, and the gunner, also a corporal. A movement beside a small rise to their left made Ken reach for his binoculars. An Iraqi infantryman was raising a rocket-propelled grenade launcher, taking aim directly at the gun truck.

In a split-second came a violent blast and deafening thunder. Smoke and flames seeped out of the engine.

Kenneth Lively jerked his head to the left and a bullet pierced his upper arm. More rounds hammered against the armored vehicle. The young soldier driver next to him slumped forward, shot through the neck. The gunner, behind them, a farm boy from Sioux City, Iowa, died instantly.

As the flames licked the edge of the hood and crept toward the windshield, Ken struggled with one hand to open the door, but he couldn't grasp the scorching handle. Heat seared his face and throat. He felt himself losing consciousness.

When more bullets pinged off the right side of the vehicle, he glanced to the three o'clock direction. In one quick motion, he shoved the window back, lifted his M4, flipped it to automatic, and fired. The Iraqi rifleman went down.

Smoke and fire poured out of the engine when, out of nowhere, sprang First Sergeant Gordon Meese. He pulled Ken Lively out of the Humvee and slung him over his shoulder. Gordon staggered toward safety about ten yards before an explosion dropped them both to the ground.

Ken raised his head to see the armored vehicle flung on its side, as flames engulfed it from all corners.

Gordon grabbed him by the collar and dragged him the rest of the way, while bullets peppered the ground all around them.

He didn't remember anything after that, but found out later Gordon, with the assistance of an Army medic, carried him to an aid station where he was subsequently transported to the rear and evacuated.

I OWE GORDON my life, Ken thought. A blast of sandy dust brought him back to where he stood leaning against the wind as it roared across Rinker Road. He turned his gaze to the highway.

Another army of tumbleweeds cascaded down the paved road, bouncing into and around vehicles unfortunate enough to be in their path. When Ken recognized Gordon's Jeep, with several tumbleweeds dragging beneath the frame and remnants of the cursed weed hanging from its sides, he chuckled and walked down to the road. He kept his arm raised to shield his face from the wind.

Following an assignment at Fort Sill, Oklahoma—340 miles east of Clayton, Ken had left the Army and joined Gordon in the northeast corner of New Mexico. They spent long hours together at nearby hunting and fishing grounds. Gordon was settled in at the land office by then, and Ken found work as a surveyor in Texline, Texas, beside the New Mexico state line.

Ken was an Ichabod Crane type of fellow. Tall and thin with a slight stoop, he had long ago lost his erect military posture. His Adam's apple bounced up and down when he spoke.

GORDON TURNED OFF the highway and parked behind the F150. As he trudged toward Ken, he brushed strands of tumbleweed off his clothes with his work gloves. "Jesus, Mary, and Joseph! I've never driven through anything like that in my life."

"This morning's paper is calling it 'The Great Tumbleweed Migration,'" Ken said.

"Good name for it. Friggin' unreal." Gordon turned his head and coughed. "I did some research on these goddamn weeds a while back. Seems they first arrived in this country in 1877 when a group of Russian immigrant farmers received a shipment of flax seeds from home. These damned thistles piggybacked a ride. Now we've got goddamn tumbleweeds rolling and tumbling throughout the West. A single tumbleweed can carry 250,000 seeds, for Christ's sake!"

"And mean damn stickers," Ken said. He pointed to a tumbleweed stuck between two telephone pole guy-wires. "Look at that one. Size of a VW beetle."

Gordon coughed again. "Any luck finding those state markers?"

Ken nodded to his left. "Found one over there."

"The hell you did!"

"Follow me." Ken turned and walked up the small rise.

Gordon trudged behind him. He wiped his mouth with the back of his hand. "Good work, Kenneth, my boy!"

Ken stopped and pointed down at the marker. "This is the northwest corner of the Texas panhandle where New Mexico meets Texas." He poked his thumb to the east. "On down this dirt road, through that house-sized mass of Russian thistle, is the other one. They mark the northern boundary of the almost three-mile-wide strip of land that's part of Texas."

"But belongs to New Mexico."

Gordon reminded his friend that after it established the Territory of New Mexico in 1850, Congress hired a surveyor named John H. Clark to set its eastern border along the 103rd meridian. That was in 1859. "The border follows the 103rd beside Oklahoma, then jumps west of the meridian along Texas."

"Yup. I know." Ken poked Gordon in the ribs. "That's what you and I are looking at right now, Sarge."

Gordon ignored the comment. "That error extends from the 36.5 parallel in the north to the 32nd parallel in the south."

"What's the basis for the error?" Ken squinted in the bright sun.

"Well, the longitude reference used by Congress in 1850 was the Washington meridian, the north/south line bisecting the dome of the old Naval Observatory in Washington, D.C. There's speculation that Clark used the Washington meridian as his reference, not the Greenwich Meridian which the United States adopted in 1912."

"I'll be damned." Ken rubbed his chin. "I have another question, professor."

"Shoot."

"What's the difference in longitude between the two reference points?"

"I've asked the folks with U.S. Geological Service, and I'm not sure even they have an answer," Gordon said. "But, therein, Kenneth, my boy, rests one of the sources of lots of arguments, land disputes, political chicanery, and fistfights. You name it. A lot of second and third generation folks in eastern New Mexico are still pissed about that contested strip of land. Some brush it off as 'the surveying error of 1859.' Others claim President William Howard Taft didn't question the discrepancy when granting New Mexico statehood in 1912, because a Yale classmate owned ranching property along the west Texas border. Can you believe it?"

"Yeah, I can believe it. It's spelled politics, Sarge. " Ken chuckled. "I figured politics and politicians had to be in there someplace. William Howard Taft, eh?"

"Yup. Looking out for his whiffenpoof Yalie friend." Gordon scratched his whiskered chin and grinned. "Then there are those who just enjoy a good argument and an excuse to toss back another shot of José Cuervo to start one."

He turned and pointed west at Rabbit Ears Mountain. "I've got something else for you."

Ken shook his head and grinned. "Sarge, you're a piece of work."

"Clayton Lake is over there to the left of Rabbit Ears."

"Uh-huh." Ken squinted his eyes again and peered at Gordon.

"We've both seen some of those dinosaur tracks that were discovered back in the fifties."

"Many times. What does that have to do with anything?" Ken said.

"I did some research on the Western Interior Seaway recently. One hundred million years ago, it covered much of the central part of America's western land area. What would one day become New Mexico's eastern boundary was under water. Lots of water. It remained so for another 30 million years until it receded with the rise of the Rocky Mountains."

Ken chuckled. "Hell, you were just a kid then."

"Smartass." Gordon said. "The 103rd meridian, which should be New Mexico's eastern border, was created long after the disappearance of the Seaway. The 103rd extends from the North Pole to the South Pole through North Dakota, South Dakota, Nebraska, Colorado, the New Mexico/Oklahoma border, and Texas."

"You missed your calling, Gordon," Ken said. "You should be in a classroom, for Christ's sake."

"Let me tell you about the dinosaurs." He looked toward Rabbit Ears Mountain. "At lunch I read a report that stated close to 800 footprints have been found since their original discovery. Can you believe it? Those big dudes had a pathway from Tucumcari clear to Fort Collins." Gordon flicked a stray tumbleweed stem off the top of his head. "Speaking of pathways, did you bring the map?"

"Yep, I got it. That's interesting about the dinosaur tracks." Ken glanced up at the gray sky. "Let's get inside my pickup, out of this damned wind."

They walked toward the truck. "Does anyone in Texline know you're working with me?" Gordon said.

"Yeah, but they don't care. New Mexico has been trying to get this strip of land back for a century and a half. They figure you're just pissin' up a rope like all the others."

"That's what they think, huh?" Gordon kicked at a stone with the toe of his work boot.

"Down deep, most Texans who are aware of the dispute know it should probably be in New Mexico. But, have you any idea how many oil derricks and water wells there are within that three-mile strip?"

"A bunch, I suspect."

"You damned right there are," Ken said. "Politicians in Austin have no intention of giving that land back. Can't say as I blame 'em."

"What the hell do you mean you can't blame 'em?" Gordon growled.

"They'd probably be voted out of office if they favored giving up that territory. 'Sides which, I'm having fun watching you dig into this little bit of history."

Gordon said nothing for a little while. "Pissin' up a rope, huh?" he grunted. He looked to the south at the flat Texas horizon.

Ken followed his gaze. "What are you going to do with this?"

Gordon paused. "Kenneth, with the exception of these goddamn Russian thistles—which violate borders at will—everything else has its boundaries: people, animals, countries, states. Everything!

"Okay, but now that you know where the markers are, what are you gonna do?"

"Let's just call this my exercise in intellectual curiosity."

"I'm not sure I know what you mean. Hell, we're in our mid-fifties. Time to start slowing down."

Gordon shook his head. "Uh-uh. Not yet."

"What do you have at stake in this dispute? You don't have any land along the border. Why should you give a shit if Texas sits on a piece of New Mexico dirt?"

"Because it just isn't right, Kenneth." There was a tremor in Gordon's voice. He turned and faced his friend. "When boundaries are violated, there are consequences. Ask Saddam Hussein about his violation of Kuwait's border in 1991." He spat on the ground.

"Saddam's dead."

Gordon reached for Ken's burned hand. "I think of that dead son of a bitch every time I look at your hand." He hesitated. "And I think of those vows we both took with our former wives, 'To love, honor, and obey.' I violated hell out of the honor boundaries by drinking myself to oblivion. Found my ass in divorce court. I seem to recall the same thing happened to you."

Ken deferred to his friend in silence. Challenging Gordon's harmless moral crusade would accomplish nothing.

They arrived at the pickup and climbed in.

"As two former Army men, you and I know all about the boundary violations that triggered two world wars, the Korean War, and Desert Storm," Gordon said.

"God works in strange ways," Ken said.

"God? You wanna talk about God? Which God? Buddha? Mohammed? Jesus Christ? Elvis? People and their 'gods' are the biggest violators of all! Like these goddamned tumbleweeds. They know no fucking boundaries. Their mullahs and their popes fan the flames of fanaticism for control of people's minds and people's purses!"

Gordon stared at Ken. "Can't you see that, Kenneth? The creed of those sonsabitches is: I'm right. Everyone else is wrong. Pass the collection basket."

The conversation had taken a familiar turn. Prior to their near-fatal Hafar Al-Batin ambush, Gordon had been a laid-back, easygoing guy, not easily upset. Since then, however, in addition to the occasional bourbon binge, Ken witnessed more frequent moments of intense cynicism and episodes of easily triggered anger from Gordon.

His concern made him search for information about PTSD and he found that post-traumatic stress disorder was a relatively new term. During World War I they called it shell shock. In World War II it was battle fatigue. PTSD became the term following the Vietnam War.

Ken placed his hand on Gordon's arm. "Sorry I got you wound up, Sarge."

"Wound up, my ass!" Gordon took a deep breath. "Goddammit, ever since I was a kid in eastern New Mexico and saw this crooked line on the state map, I wanted to know why. Why wasn't it a straight line? Whose territory was being violated? Later I learned that John Clark screwed up."

Kenneth rested his fingers on the bottom of the pickup steering wheel. "A friend of mine told me one time it's always easy to blame a mistake on a fella who isn't around to defend himself."

"Your friend had a point," Gordon said. "And to be

fair, I'm not totally convinced Clark was in the wrong, but it certainly appears he was. Be that as it may, will Texas acknowledge the error? Hell no!"

"Why wasn't the error corrected back then?"

"Lost its priority when the Civil War started in 1861." Gordon scratched his chin. "Nonetheless, in my mind, the state of Texas is guilty of violating New Mexico's border by asserting that no surveying error ever occurred. And you don't need to call me Sarge."

Kenneth nodded.

Gordon pushed at the nosepiece of his glasses. "To answer your earlier question—'What am I going to do with this?'—I'm going to jump in my Skyhawk some night, with a New Mexico flag, and fly down to the 103rd meridian where it intersects 32 degrees latitude, and I'm going to plant the goddamn flag! That is where I'm going with this."

"You're serious?"

"Fuckin' right, I'm serious!" He turned red.

Ken chuckled. "You sound like my former mother-in-law."

"Screw you."

With windows and doors closed, they felt the wind pushing against the side of the truck.

"Back to the markers and monuments." Ken reached behind the seat and pulled the map from a cardboard box. He unfolded it across their laps. "That's why we're out here, right?" With the tip of his pen he pointed at a spot. "Here's where we are right now. And here are the two markers."

Gordon nodded. "Okay." He had quieted down from

his earlier outburst. On the map, he ran his finger up the Texas panhandle and stopped at the narrow strip of Oklahoma resting above Texas. "The Oklahoma panhandle is interesting, isn't it?"

"Yeah, it is. That sliver of land is called *No Man's Land*. It's bordered by Kansas, Colorado, New Mexico, and Texas and it juts out like a finger, pointing west from what was once the Indian Territory. There was a time no one wanted it and no one claimed it. According to a Park Ranger friend of mine over at Fort Union, it got its moniker *No Man's Land* back in the 1800s when Texas decided to relinquish claim to the territory and it became part of Oklahoma." Ken looked across the pickup's hood toward the eastern edge of Oklahoma's panhandle. "Outlaws loved that wedge of dirt. Outlaws like Silas Hampton, Alphonso Jennings, and Sam McWilliams to name a few. They could hide out as long as they wanted and no one was around to put `em in jail."

Ken started the engine and drove toward the east corner marker. In the distance, lightning and black sky bore signs of possible tornado activity.

"Let's put it off for now," Gordon said. "I don't like the looks of this. We can check it out another time."

"No. We're almost there. See that corner where the road turns ninety degrees north? That's Oklahoma. To the right of the corner is the other marker."

After a short distance Ken stopped the truck and pointed at a four-foot-high concrete monument behind a barbed wire fence. It stood as a lonely sentinel in the wild and fertile grassland. "There it is—where the Oklahoma state line meets the Texas panhandle."

They got out of the truck and, in the blistering wind, read the bronze plate atop the monument: U.S. General Land Office Survey, 1932.

Gordon rubbed his hands together. "Bigger than hell! I've got business to take care of in Santa Fe tomorrow. While I'm there, I'll see what I can find in the state archives."

Thunder rumbled and the sky turned black.

"Take me back to my Jeep and let's get the hell out of here."

CHAPTER 3

While Gordon and Ken identified boundary monuments and state lines, Ty Daggett and Henry Lewis were enjoying center-cut sirloin steaks at the Rabbit Ear Café. Their table was against the parking lot window.

"So your three-year-old colt isn't broke yet?" Ty asked.

Henry shook his head. "I haven't had time to break him. Just haven't had time. And I'm not as young as I used to be, Ty." He stroked his bushy gray moustache. "How long does it take you to break a horse?"

"Oh, to fully break one where we totally know each other, maybe a year or two. But to get a horse green broke—around 30 days." He took a sip of coffee. "The colt's a gelding?"

"He is."

Ty looked down at the stainless steel fork on the table and turned it over in his hand. "You're asking a fair price."

"I've seen you train a few horses. You have a way with them. And you're gentler than a lot of men are."

"I guess we all have our ways of doing things, Henry.

When I'm working with a horse, trust is the key; we've got to trust each other. Punishment is never a consideration. A horse reads punishment as a betrayal of trust."

"I saw a guy in Santa Fe, one time, trying to break a young horse," Henry said. "He whipped the poor animal across the head with a bridle. A mean, evil spirited SOB."

"Did you take him on?" Ty said.

"Oh, yeah... I won't put up with that crap." He pushed his hat to the back of his head with his gnarled fingers. "I've never forgiven the son of a bitch. Thrashed his sorry ass."

It had been nearly a year since Henry Lewis and his wife, Clara, moved from Farmington, on the other side of the state, to Clayton, after his younger brother, Edward, died. Colon cancer killed him. Their widowed mother tried to run the Lewis ranch by herself with the help of two part-time cowboys until it became too much for her. Henry and Clara made the decision to sell their Farmington operation and move to Clayton to take over.

The Lewis property line had joined the Daggett family ranch for at least three generations, an arrangement which benefitted both families, particularly so at branding time or during roundups, when extra hands were needed. Access to each of the spreads was gained by dirt ranch roads off the highway between Clayton and Nara Visa, just west of the New Mexico/Texas state line. A two-rutted road ran for close to three miles between the Daggett and the Lewis farm houses.

Sarah Jane filled their coffee cups while Henry glanced out at the parking lot. He turned back and stirred in some cream in his cup. "You ever miss your Air Force days, Ty?"

"I enjoyed my time there." Ty cut a slice of the sirloin. "I think back on it every once in a while. Worked with a lot of fine people."

"You've become a good rancher."

"Thanks." Ty smiled at the way Henry sometimes treated him like a son. He chewed on the steak and thought for a moment. "Ranching's a tough, but rewarding business. No boss to answer to and no clock to punch." He cut another slice. "No office politics or employer to please."

"But we earn our keep, Ty. We earn our keep."

"Damn right we do."

Nearby, the dark-haired woman in the broomstick skirt paid her lunch bill. The cashier took her credit card. The name on the card read *Alysa Cody*. She signed the receipt, then walked to the door.

Ty gave the lady a courtly nod as she walked by their table. She smiled at both men.

"Nice-looking lady," Ty said.

"Mm-hmm." Henry nodded.

With the noon hour long past, only a few other tables were occupied. At one table not far from the door sat two elderly women in jeans and work shirts. The eldest, with solid white hair, wore a faded cowboy hat sporting a black raven feather.

"Will the colt take a halter?" said Ty.

"Oh, yeah. I've trained him that far."

Ty reached across the table. "I'll buy him." They shook hands. "I need a young horse. Hannibal is starting to slow down, as you've probably noticed. Comin' up on eighteen years."

Henry nodded. "Hannibal is a prize horse, Ty. A prize horse."

Ty pushed his plate to the side. "I don't want to try getting the colt into a trailer quite yet, so I'll ride Hannibal over in the morning and lead him back to my place."

Henry reached for his wallet and stood up. "I'll pay for lunch."

THE TWO RANCHERS stepped outside the restaurant as Alysa Cody walked across the parking lot toward her car. They watched while she stopped, waiting for a late model SUV entering the lot to pass. The vehicle came to a halt in front of her.

"What do you suppose is going on?" Henry moved his hat back to the front of his head.

"I don't know," Ty murmured. His eyes focused on the scene from beneath his Stetson. "It's none of our business. But I don't like the looks of it."

A middle-aged man in a business suit got out of the SUV and approached Alysa. "Did you get my text?"

"Yes," Alysa said. Her face reddened.

"And?" Michael Cody said.

"I think you are a coward. You don't have the spine to ask me for a divorce to my face." She glanced at the woman seated in his car. "And I think you're a selfish, sickening, horny old fool."

He looked down at his feet. "I don't want a scene,

Alysa." He cleared his throat. "I'm sorry it didn't work out."

She didn't respond.

Cody glanced at the blonde in the car, then back at Alysa. "I hope we can settle things without a costly fight. Lawyers aren't cheap."

She stared at him. "I'm thirty-five now, and I've come a long way from my family's farm in Bryan. I supported you during your internship and residency and helped you establish your successful medical practice back in Gatesville. We've recently purchased a second home here." She paused. "I won't fight with you, Michael. Or for you. You're not worth it. But I will demand a fair settlement."

She turned to leave and Michael grabbed her arm. "I want a fast divorce," he snapped.

"What's the rush? That chick in the car?" She tried to break free and he pulled her back.

Henry and Ty strode across the parking lot toward the couple.

Michael's jaw tightened. He squeezed her arm and started to reply until he saw the two ranchers approaching. He released his hold.

"Anything we can do to help?" Ty said. He hooked his thumbs over his black leather belt.

"Yeah, you can mind your own business." Michael Cody ran the palm of his hand along the side of his head, patted his slick black hair, then ran a finger over a narrow moustache. The SUV engine was running.

"Is that so?" Ty glanced at Alysa. "Are you all right, ma'am?"

"Like I said," Cody narrowed his eyes, "you and your friend can go about your business. I'm just talking to my wife."

Alysa glanced at the two ranchers. She clasped her hands and stepped back.

Ty stood a good six inches taller than the man in the suit. He looked down at him. "Sir, my friend and I will go about our business in due course. But you happen to be in this cafe's parking lot and, in my opinion, you are being discourteous to this lady. That makes it our business."

Cody stared at Alysa, then up at Ty Daggett. "To hell with all of you." He turned, got in his SUV, slammed the door, and started the engine. The young woman in the passenger seat said something. He ignored her.

As the man sped away, Ty noted the Texas license plate and chrome Gatesville Texas frame. He ran the back of his hand across his chin and wondered what brought these folks, especially this lovely young lady, from Gatesville to Clayton.

"Thank you," Alysa said in a soft voice.

Ty tipped his hat to her and turned around to rejoin Henry, who had waited behind him. He caught the twinkle in Henry's eyes. "What are you grinning at?"

Henry nudged him in the arm as they walked toward their trucks. "Did you get her phone number?"

Ty halted. "What do you mean?"

"How long has it been since you've seen a woman as pretty as that?" Henry chuckled. "Yessirree, she's mighty pretty, didn't you say so yourself?"

"What if I did?"

"Well, I just thought, you being single and all, you might feel the urge to—"

Ty laid an arm across Henry's shoulder. "In case you didn't notice, I've got a ranch to run." He climbed into his truck and inserted the key into the ignition, but didn't turn it. He sat in silence and replayed the scene.

Maybe he had felt the urge to protect her.

CHAPTER 4

At noon the following day, Gordon Meese drove to the Rabbit Ear in his old Willys. He sat at the same table as the day before and lingered over lunch. There was no sign of the woman he had seen the day before.

He was halfway through lunch when a group of six people, men and women, entered the restaurant. They were seated at the table beside his. Sarah Jane, the waitress, took their drink orders and asked where they were from. One of the men said, "We're from Amarillo. Just passing through Clayton. We heard good things about this place."

"Thank you," Sarah Jane said. "We appreciate your stopping to see us."

When Sarah Jane returned with their drinks, Gordon watched as the Texas tourists passed a map of some kind around the table and laughed. One of the men showed Sarah Jane the map.

She examined it and joined their laughter. "I've never seen a map of the United States like this. Good heavens!" She laughed again.

The man noticed Gordon observing the activity. He leaned over and smiled. "Sir, would you like to see this?"

He handed Gordon the 8 ½ x 11 inch map, a cartoonist's rendering of the United States with the State of Texas occupying more than half of the country's land mass. New Mexico was but a narrow sliver of land.

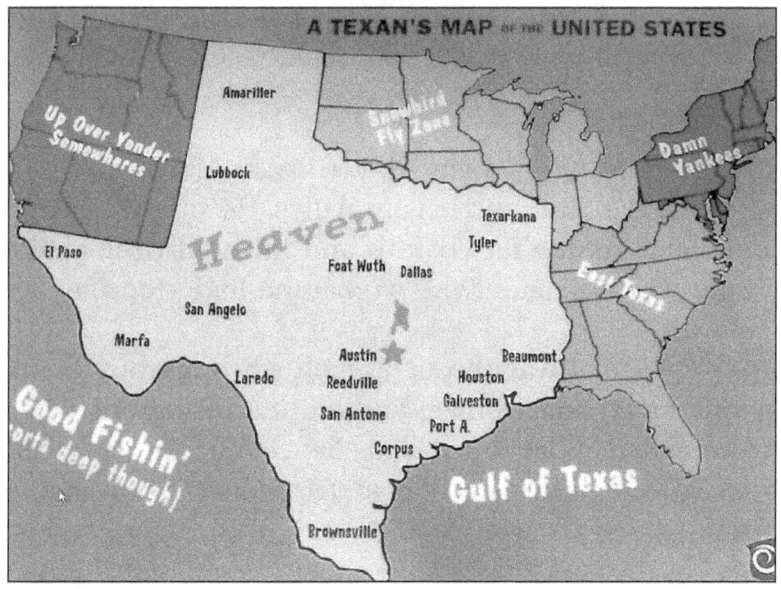

Gordon studied the cartoon then looked up, without expression.

The Amarillo man was still smiling. "Do you like it?"

Gordon's face reddened. "You people think this is funny?"

"Yes, sir," the man said. He glanced at the colorful map in Gordon's hands then looked back at Gordon. "We do. I guess I hoped you would as well."

"I think it is pretty goddamn offensive."

"Offensive in what way?" The man sat back. "I didn't mean to upset you, sir."

The other guests from Amarillo, sensing the sudden tension in the air, became silent and turned to Gordon.

"In what way, you ask?" Gordon's voice rose. "You bastards stole six hundred thousand acres of land from New Mexico. Land along the 103rd meridian. And," he glared at the man, "you think this goddamn map is funny, for Christ's sake!"

Out of the corner of his eye, Gordon noticed Sarah Jane dart to the manager's desk behind the cashier's stand. The restaurant became silent as all heads turned toward the confrontation.

The man reached for the map and Gordon released it as he glanced up to see the restaurant manager approaching. A man ten years younger and fifty pounds heavier than Gordon.

"What's going on here?" the manager said.

The man from Amarillo turned. "Just a misunderstanding."

"Misunderstanding, my ass!" Gordon shouted. "You Texans stole land from New Mexico, goddamnit!"

No sooner had the words left Gordon's mouth than the husky manager's hand gripped his arm. "I won't put up with this kind of behavior in this establishment, sir. From anyone." In his other hand was the bill for Gordon's lunch. "Come with me. You will pay your bill and leave."

As he marched Gordon past Sarah Jane, the manager said, "The restaurant will pick up the tab for that table."

Angry and chagrined, Gordon left the café, got in the Jeep, and drove to Santa Fe, 214 miles to the southwest.

HIS FIRST STOP in Santa Fe was the barbershop owned by Santiago Luna, an old friend who threatened to double his price for the haircut. "Where the hell you been living, Meese?" he said. "In a cave?"

"I haven't had time for a haircut," Gordon groused. "Been too busy." He took off his glasses and slipped them in a shirt pocket.

"Too busy?" Santiago snapped the barber cape over Gordon's shirt collar. "I thought you retired up there in Logan or Clayton."

"I did. Logan."

"So, what's the difference?" Santiago took a step back to study the cut in the large mirror. "I never been up there."

"Logan is an hour-and-a-half south of Clayton."

"Bueno." Santiago ran a comb through Gordon's gray hair. "So what are you busy with, hombre?" He resumed cutting with the same stainless steel scissors he'd been using since barber school. "You rustling cattle or something? Going across the state line into Texas? Herding 'em across the border to New Mexico?"

Two other customers, both reading newspapers, sat in chairs facing the shop's three barber chairs. They glanced up, amusement on their faces.

"Wish to hell I was."

"My wife's brother got caught rustling some steers up near Cimarron."

"No kidding?"

Locks and strands of Gordon's gray hair slid down the black-and-white striped cape to the checkerboard parquet floor. "Now he's in the state pen for a couple of years. Stupid bastard." He rotated the chair one way, then the other, cutting and chattering all the while. "When you gonna get married, Gordon?"

"Tried it once."

"I'm on my third wife." The scissor clips took on a rhythm. "Third time's the charm." He swung the chair around to face the mirror. "Well, boss, what do you think?"

Gordon studied the haircut in the wall-sized mirror. "Looks a lot better than when I got in the chair, amigo."

Santiago removed the striped cape. "Bueno, Meese. Now you're ready to go find another wife."

Gordon handed him a $20 bill. "Not likely, Santiago. I'll see you next time I'm in town."

THE NEW MEXICO Historical Archives office was Gordon's next stop where, after providing satisfactory identification and signing in, he met with the senior staff archivist, Art Duran, a middle-aged man with a firm handshake.

"I'm looking for information on the 103rd meridian," Gordon said.

"Ah, one of my favorite subjects—the 103rd."

"Why is that?"

"Well, that line, extending from the North Pole to the South Pole, raises all kinds of havoc along the New Mexico/Texas border."

"I'm aware of that."

"I figured you might be." Art winked.

Over Art's shoulder, Gordon noticed an elderly couple, likely married, the only other visitors present. Seated side by side at a small table, the woman held a magnifying glass in her hand as they studied the contents of an accordion file.

Art tilted his head. "That couple comes in at least once a week. She's a retired history professor from UNM down in Albuquerque. Loves to research New Mexico history."

"What about him?"

"He just tags along. They're a very close couple."

"Nice."

Art pointed to a long rectangular conference table on the opposite side of the room. "Let's sit over there."

They walked to the table and pulled out chairs on opposite sides. Bookcases, filled to capacity, lined the two side walls of the large room. Gordon removed the spiral notepad from his shirt pocket.

"The last time someone asked me about the boundary discrepancy was when the Texas Land Commissioner issued a challenge to the New Mexico Land Commissioner to settle the dispute with an old-fashioned duel."

Gordon laughed. "No kidding? When was that?"

"Not too long ago." Art scratched his head. "I think it was in 2003."

"That's wild!"

"And they were both Republicans!" He chuckled.

"Who won?"

"They cancelled it. Wish they hadn't. Our guy is a real cowboy. He can handle a horse and a pistol!"

"How much land are we talking about?"

Art scratched his head. "That strip of real estate contains 603,485 acres."

"That's a lot of dirt and a chunk of tax revenue to whoever owns it."

"You're right about that." He stood. "I think I know what you're looking for. I'll be right back."

Gordon glanced at the retired couple across the room. The woman pointed to a document while the man shook his head and asked her for the magnifying glass. He studied the piece of paper and took some notes. Then they gathered their things and picked up the accordion file and walked to the front desk. The man was slightly bent over.

Gordon watched as he took the woman's arm. They were an attractive couple; reminded him of his grandparents when he was a kid. The woman handed the file to the receptionist and they left.

Fifteen minutes passed. An elevator door opened. Art emerged pushing a small stainless steel table on wheels. On the table sat a cardboard banker's box with a pair of white cotton gloves resting on its top.

He handed the gloves to Gordon. "Here, put these on."

"What for?"

"You're going to be handling some very old documents and maps. We don't want the oil from your fingers damaging them. Everything we have in these archives is of historic value. We have to be extremely careful. You and I, human beings, often do the greatest harm."

Gordon raised his eyebrows. "Because of oil from our skin?"

"Oil, sweat, make-up." He rested his hand on the box. "I'll be in my office if you need anything."

Once he was seated at the conference table, Gordon removed the box cover. The cavernous room was silent except for the low hum of an air conditioning unit. Inside the box were several folders with maps, letters, documents—many of them yellowed with age. The first document he held in his gloved hands was a letter dated March 12, 1906, from W.A. Richards, Land Office Commissioner, Department of The Interior, Washington, D.C., to the Honorable H.J. Hagerman, Territorial Governor of New Mexico. The letter concluded with a statement that until Congress considered further legislation regarding the disputed strip of land between New Mexico and Texas, the Interior Department would continue to recognize the existing boundaries.

Gordon shook his head. "Politics. Goddamn politics!"

He set the letter aside, then reached back in the box and retrieved several more letters and memoranda. He studied each item and returned it to the box. As he picked up the box cover to replace it, a folded document stuck against the bottom of the box, beneath the manila file folders, caught his eye.

He lifted the folders from the box and set them to the side. Then he removed one of his cotton gloves and slowly peeled the fragile document away from the box bottom with his fingernails. When it broke free, he set it on the conference table and carefully unfolded it. It was a hand-drawn surveyor's diagram delineating the Texas, Oklahoma, and New Mexico territorial/state boundaries. The diagram included the Texas/New Mexico surveying discrepancies in precise detail as of December 20th, 1903.

E
m.J.P.

38764-1906

DEPARTMENT OF THE INTERIOR

GENERAL LAND OFFICE,

WASHINGTON, D. C.,

ADDRESS ONLY THE
COMMISSIONER OF THE GENERAL LAND OFFICE.

March 12, 1906.

Hon. H. J. Hagerman,

    Santa Fe, New Mexico.

Sir:

    I am in receipt of your letter dated, February 27, 1906, requesting such information as will show you the exact status of the Texas-New Mexico boundary question.

    You state that the people in the vicinity of Texico and at other points along the doubtful line are in a very uncertain and unsatisfactory state of mind and that they and other people in other parts of the country, whom land agents are trying to get to settle on the disputed strip, have made frequent inquiries of you in regard to it and you ask for such information in regard to the matter as may be furnished you.

    In reply, you are advised that the boundary lines established between New Mexico and Texas in 1859-60, by the Boundary Commission, under the act of June 5, 1856 (11 Stats., 310) were confirmed as the true boundary lines by the act of Congress approved March 3, 1891 (26 Stats., 971). These lines were established by a Boundary Commission upon which John H. Clark was appointed as commissioner on behalf of the United States and the lines established have usually been referred to as the "Clark Lines." The

2

32nd parallel of north latitude was first established as the south boundary of New Mexico from a point on the Rio Grande to the one hundred and third meridian , west longitude, which latter formed the east boundary of the territory. Portions only of this meridian were actually established and marked in the field, that between the 32nd and 33rd parallels of latitude from the south end of the meridian and that from the northwest corner of Texas (latitude 36° 30') south as far as the 34th parallel, leaving a distance of some seventy miles not marked in any manner.

Public land surveys have recently been made in the locality of Texico and in these surveys the conditions along that part of the 103d meridian have been found to be in accordance with previous general reports concerning the same, i.e., although no Clark monuments were found in that locality, a line of fence, known as the "Syndicate fence" had been constructed by parties owning land in Texas as the west boundary of their holdings, and while this fence could not be considered as an official line, yet it was found to be in the position where other surveys referred to Clark monuments to the north would indicate its existence as approximately defining the line established by Clark.

Under authority from the Secretary of the Interior, an investigation was made of these boundary lines and of the 100th meridian by Arthur D. Kidder, Examiner of Surveys of this office in 1903, with a view of determining the astronomical locations of the various lines defining the common boundaries of New Mexico

3

and Texas, and a report thereon was submitted April 19, 1904, to the Secretary of the Interior, with the view to having the same submitted to Congress, as a basis for such further legislation if any as might be deemed necessary to define with exactness these boundaries upon the ground. So far no such legislation has been had.

It was found by Mr. Kidder that at the intersection of the parallels defined as the boundaries that there were discrepancies between the Clark survey of the 103d meridian and the Kidder location thereof varying from 2.7 miles at the northwest corner of Texas to 3.84 miles at the southeast corner of New Mexico.

Until further legislation is had, this office will continue to recognize the Clark lines as establishing the east and south boundaries of New Mexico.

Very respectfully,

W. A. Richards

Commissioner.

L.J.

The New Mexico Commission of Public Records has granted permission to reprint the following archived documents:

From the Gov. William McDonald Papers, Collection No. 1959-094, Box SN 17249, folder 421, New Mexico State Archives.

"Three-page letter, dated March 12, 1906, from U.S. Department on the Interior to H. J. Hagerman"

At the bottom of the page was a calligraphic text describing its content "… as determined by Arthur D. Kidder, Examiner of Surveys." The difference between the "present Texas-New Mexico Bdy (Clark's location, 1859)" and "True 103rd Meridian" was clearly displayed.

"Holy crap! This is just what I was looking for!" Gordon rose from the table and walked to Art Duran's office. "Any chance I can photocopy a couple of these documents?"

"Sure, I'll do it for you." Art took off his horn-rimmed glasses and set them on his desk. "Come on."

Gordon followed him to a large photocopying machine in an adjacent room.

Art picked up the map, examined it, and stopped. "Where did you find this?"

"It was stuck to the bottom of the box."

Art slipped on a pair of cotton gloves and spread the map on top of the photocopy machine. "This, my friend, is a treasure. A definite key to the boundary dispute. We were afraid it was lost."

"Will it help settle the dispute?"

"I'm afraid not. It is of value to archivists and historians." Art arched his eyebrows. "But there's no way in hell Texas will cede that land. With all that oil and water? No way in hell. I'm grateful to you for finding it."

"Is it okay if I have a photocopy of this, too?"

"Of course." Art examined the sketch and ran his gloved fingers across it. "But first let me point something out to you."

Gordon leaned over Art's shoulder.

"Some people call the boundary error between

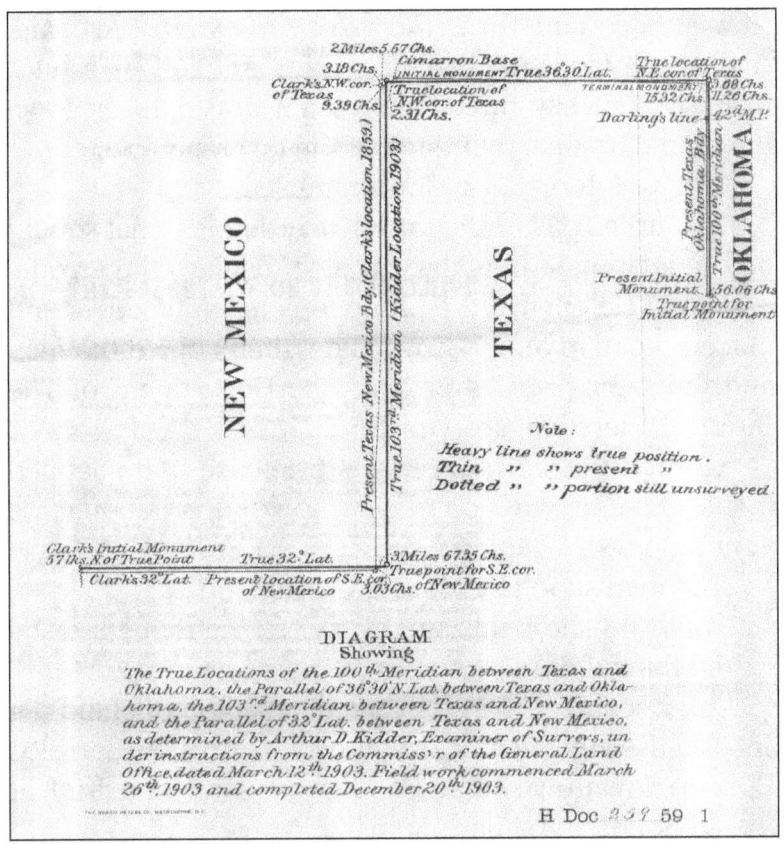

DIAGRAM
Showing

The True Locations of the 100 th Meridian between Texas and
Oklahoma, the Parallel of 36°30'N Lat, between Texas and Oklahoma, the 103 rd Meridian between Texas and New Mexico,
and the Parallel of 32° Lat, between Texas and New Mexico,
as determined by Arthur D. Kidder, Examiner of Surveys, under instructions from the Commiss'r of the General Land
Office, dated March 12 th 1903. Field work commenced March
26 th 1903 and completed December 20 th 1903.

H Doc 259 59 1

The New Mexico Commission of Public Records has granted permission to reprint the following archived documents:

From the Gov. William McDonald Papers, Collection No. 1959-094, Box SN 17249, folder 521, New Mexico State Archives.

> "Texas, New Mexico, and Oklahoma Boundary Lines, Letter from the Secretary of the Interior transmitting the Report of the Astronomical Investigations of the Texas, New Mexico, and Oklahoma Boundary Line, Dec. 19, 1905. Document No. 259, House of Representatives, 59th Congress, First Session"

New Mexico and Texas *the three-mile strip*." Art said. "Others say *two-and-a-half miles*. Actually it ranges from two miles to three." He ran his gloved finger down the boundary line, pointing out the discrepancies.

"That's interesting," Gordon mused.

Art turned. "This diagram clearly defines what should be the legitimate boundary; it also displays the erroneous one." He opened the photocopy machine cover and placed the map on the glass plate, then copied the map and the three-page letter from the Department of The Interior. "Here you are, Gordon."

Gordon placed them in his briefcase and snapped it shut. "Damn, you don't know how much I appreciate your help, Art. Thank you."

The men shook hands and Gordon left.

Wait 'til I show this survey to Ken, he thought as he exited the building.

After securing the briefcase in a lockbox behind the Jeep's passenger seat, Gordon drove north on Cerrillos Road to downtown Santa Fe. He was ready for a drink at the La Fonda Hotel bar.

The sun shone down on the old town beneath a turquoise blue sky and scattered white clouds. He turned east on San Francisco Street, two blocks from the La Fonda, and slowed for a car backing into a parking spot. Glancing at the pedestrians on the sidewalk to his left, he caught his breath.

Walking toward him was the woman he'd seen at the Rabbit Ear two days earlier. The woman who reminded him of Molly. He hoped she'd turn so he could wave or smile—any kind of acknowledgment. *Please.*

The driver behind him interrupted his reverie by sitting on his horn.

"Crap!" In the left side mirror he could see the mystery woman continuing in the opposite direction.

No more street side parking spots. Another glance at the mirror. She was gone. "Damn!"

He remembered a municipal parking lot one block south. He spun the steering wheel to the right at Don Gaspar Avenue. As soon as he rounded the corner, a party of tourists dawdled across the narrow street. Gordon jammed his boot against the brake pedal, stopping just short of them.

"Jesus Christ!" He gripped the steering wheel, breathed deeply, and exhaled.

The last pedestrian, a small wizened man wearing a brightly colored Hawaiian shirt and using a cane, stopped in the middle of the street and stared at Gordon. He shook his head then turned and joined the others. Gordon, on the brink of flipping the senior citizen a bird, gritted his teeth and proceeded to the municipal lot.

He found an empty spot in the back row of the lot and returned at a near run to San Francisco Street. For thirty minutes he searched every retail store and restaurant on the street.

Tia Sophia's restaurant was packed. He asked the hostess if he could look for someone who might be seated at one of the tables or booths.

"Go ahead."

He was almost embarrassed as he scoured the dining area as if on a search-and-rescue mission. He didn't know the mystery lady's name, where she lived, where she worked—nothing about her. Only that she was drop-dead beautiful and, when he saw her in Clayton, was in a world of hurt. She was Molly two decades ago.

What would he do if he *did* find her? What would he *say*? He didn't know. But he did know he was a gray-haired old guy who was acting like a pre-pubescent fool.

Gordon walked out of the restaurant, looked up and down the street one last time, and resigned himself to abandoning the search. He shoved his hands into the pockets of his khaki pants and continued down the street to a light post across the street from the Hilton Hotel. Leaning against the post, he stared absent-mindedly at the Sangre de Cristo Mountains to the east. The mountain range, with its piñon and juniper trees, rose from Santa Fe's 7,000 feet to higher elevations, its texture softening in layers of bluish gray. He pictured the top—10,000 feet—the Santa Fe Ski Basin surround-ed by aspens and sky-reaching Ponderosa pines. After a few moments he puffed up his cheeks, exhaled, and turned toward the La Fonda bar.

ON THE SECOND FLOOR of the office building, over-looking the sidewalk where Gordon sauntered, was a lawyer's office. Across the desk from the balding law-yer sat Alysa Cody, signing legal documents to initi-ate divorce proceedings against Dr. Michael Cody of Gatesville, Texas, and seeking title to their second home on the outskirts of Clayton.

She wouldn't wait long for the title. She pictured Michael Cody back in Gatesville, anxiously awaiting the documents, including the petition to the court for a final divorce decree. Michael would have his blond chickie. Alysa would have the Clayton property.

She left the lawyer's office with a narrow leather folder containing copies of the divorce documents beneath her arm. She walked down the stairs to San Francisco Street's sidewalk and turned right to the Santa Fe Plaza. As she passed a street vendor selling Chicago Dog Express hotdogs, the vendor smiled at her. She walked a few steps then turned around and came back to purchase a hot dog and a Coke.

Alysa found a park bench beneath a cottonwood tree on the east side of the Plaza and laid claim to it. She sat and placed the hot dog, wrapped in a white paper napkin, and the Coke at her side and rested the leather folder on her lap. She unwrapped the hot dog, then took a bite and thought back to the family farm in Bryan. To her childhood dreams of cities, bright lights, becoming a nurse, marrying a doctor, and raising a family. For a brief time that dream was a reality. Today she took a turn to begin the journey to a new life.

She finished eating the hot dog and drank the Coke, then walked to her car and drove to the El Rey Inn to check out. Four hours later she was back in Clayton.

When she arrived home, Alysa opened the door to what was to have been her and Michael's second home. There to greet her was her white cat, Clementine. She reached down and picked up the cat and hugged her. "You're the only one I can trust anymore, Miss Clemmie."

Early the next morning, Alysa drove to Union County General Hospital to resume her career in nursing.

CHAPTER 5

Ty Daggett slipped a check into Henry Lewis's shirt pocket. "I guess this colt is mine now, eh?" The handsome young sorrel stood beside them.

"You got yourself a good horse, Ty." Henry reached out and patted the colt's neck. "A real good horse."

From across the corral came a maternal nicker from the colt's mother. The colt pressed his ears back and snorted.

"And he hasn't held a bit yet? Or carried a saddle?"

"Not yet." Henry ran his tongue around the inside of his cheek. "That's why you're getting such a good deal."

"Humph." Ty slipped a boot into the stirrup and swung aboard Hannibal.

Henry, standing beside Hannibal, reached up and handed Ty the halter rope. The colt shook his head, trying to throw off the halter. "Got a name for him?" Henry asked.

"Trotter. He reminds me of a Cavalry horse named Trotter. Saw his picture in an old Seventh Cavalry journal a few years ago; same light-colored mane and tail as this one."

"I'll drive over from time to time and check on you and Trotter," Henry chuckled.

Ty smirked. "You do that, Henry." He glanced over his shoulder. "C'mon, boy."

TY AND THE TWO HORSES were about halfway home and descending the side of a wash into a flat, dry riverbed when his mind wandered back to his post-college years. Sandra Donovan's soft voice echoed in his head.

"NO, I CAN'T marry you, Ty. Not now, not later."

"But I've got my degree in Agricultural Economics now, and after I get out of the Air Force, I'm coming back here to ranch. My college education will pay off after all, Sandra. You'll be near your family here in Miami. We talked about this in high school, after our FFA meetings. I thought you wanted the same future I did." He took her hand in his and laced his fingers through hers.

She shook her head. "I'm sorry, I thought I did, too, but after I get my nursing degree, I'm heading off to a convent to become a nun."

"How can you do that if you love me?" He released her hand.

Tears streamed down her face, and Ty turned away so she wouldn't see the hurt in his eyes. He determined not to feel it and stalked out of the Donovan family living room to his waiting pickup.

MAYBE HE WASN'T cut out to be a husband and a

father. His own father, an unforgiving and harsh disciplinarian with a vicious temper, had not set such a loving example. Ty had always felt closer to his mother. Maybe it was her Italian genes, demonstrative and gentle at the same time. He wished he were more like her.

Ty's mind continued to wander as he and the horses rose up the other side of the wash within eyesight of the Daggett Ranch. His thoughts drifted back to the time he was a First Lieutenant stationed with the Air Force intelligence unit in Izmir, Turkey, near the end of his overseas tour.

LATE ONE AFTERNOON he received orders to report to the downtown USO office at 8:00 PM that night, an unusual directive. The office, located in downtown Izmir, was sterile and cold, with two government-issue desks, five metal chairs with vinyl seat cushions, and a file cabinet. The office had one window. Except for a framed black-and-white photograph of the theater commanding general on one of the walls, the walls were bare.

The civilian in charge, a balding man with glasses, wore a short-sleeved gray shirt and dark slacks. He had the demeanor of a movie screen mortician. A USO patch was sewn on the left sleeve of his shirt. He shook hands with Ty and asked him to take a seat in one of the two chairs in front of his desk.

He sat behind the desk. "Son, Mr. Mario Palermo, your mother's brother in Raton, New Mexico, would like to visit with you on the telephone."

"Uncle Mario?"

Nodding, he sat back in his chair. "It's early morning in Raton and he is standing by for your call. He reached us, by the way, through channels at Cannon Air Force Base at Clovis, New Mexico."

"I'm familiar with Cannon Air Force Base." Ty's brow furrowed. "What's going on?"

"It's a family matter, Lieutenant Daggett. Your mother and father have had an accident." The USO man, as cold and as sterile as the office, leaned forward with his elbows on his desk. "I'll place the call from my telephone here." He glanced at the black telephone on the desk. "And then I'll leave the office so you and your uncle can converse in private."

"Very well."

"May I proceed?"

"Of course." Ty frowned.

He placed the call through operators in Europe and the United States and waited. "Mr. Palermo?" He paused. "Lieutenant Daggett is sitting in my office."

Ty took the phone. The door closed behind the USO man. "Uncle Mario, this is Ty."

"Tyrone, my boy. It is good to hear your voice, but I have some very sad news for you. And I understand we can visit only briefly on this telephone connection."

"What is the sad news?"

"Your mother and father were killed yesterday afternoon by a terrible tornado. They were driving home from a doctor's appointment in Amarillo."

Ty placed his elbow on the desk and held his head. "What!"

"They died very quickly, Tyrone. With little suffering."

"My God, Uncle Mario… I can't believe this…"

"When I talked to the USO man earlier, he said the Air Force would arrange for you to take leave to come home for the funeral. It will be next week. I am told by a neighboring rancher that he and the other ranchers will take care of the family ranch and the livestock."

Ty's jaw tightened.

"Tyrone?"

"Yes." Ty sat up in the chair.

"We will take things one day at a time, my boy. One step at a time." He paused. "Let me know your travel schedule when you have it. I will not firm up funeral details until I hear from you."

Ty departed Izmir the next morning on an Air Force cargo plane to Frankfurt, Germany, and left Frankfurt for La Guardia the following day. From La Guardia he flew United Airlines to Albuquerque.

In view of his critical circumstances, the Air Force granted him an Honorable Discharge sixty days later. Ty shed the uniform he had worn with pride and returned home to take charge of the Daggett Ranch.

Within a few months, grief visited Ty once again with the passing of his Uncle Mario. He was on his own. But he was prepared, prepared and hardened perhaps by a stern father. He pulled on his boots, saddled Hannibal, and never looked back.

THEY ARRIVED AT the ranch midafternoon. After he unsaddled Hannibal, Ty led both horses into the pasture behind the corrals. Hannibal headed for the water trough with Trotter following closely behind. Ty closed the gate and walked to the ranch house.

The Daggett property, south of Clayton, was located at the western edge of the Great Plains and the Kiowa National Grasslands. Most of the ranch property was in New Mexico, with a small portion extending east across the state line into Texas. It was cattle country, where the green rolling grasslands of summer became buried in snow during winter.

Ty's was a cow-calf operation. His herd of Black Angus breeding cows and four or five bulls produced a calf crop each spring. Except for the 97 head of cattle, six horses, and two ranch dogs, Chico and Scooter, he lived by himself. His closest friends were neighboring ranchers and cowboys.

Chico, a black-and-white Border collie, was given to him by David Reynolds, the local veterinarian. The four-year-old dog had been abandoned at Love's Truck Stop and was taken to Doc Reynolds' kennels since Clayton had no animal shelter. Doc Reynolds named the dog, Chico, after his black and white Malamute and cared for him for three weeks. On a visit to the Daggett ranch to examine a pregnant heifer, he took Chico along. The rest was history.

Scooter, about the same age as Chico, just showed up at the ranch one day and never left. She was of unknown parentage; looked like a scruffy-haired Russell terrier. Because of her independent, sassy attitude he was going to name her Catherine the Great, but settled for Scooter. He liked the sound of the name and she seemed to like it as well. To stay on the safe side, he asked

Doc Reynolds to fix her.

HANNIBAL AND TROTTER remained in the small pasture beside the ranch corrals grazing on buffalo grass
mixed with other grasses native to the area. Ty spent
time with the colt as his work schedule permitted so
the colt could become used to his presence and his
voice. Chico and Scooter always remained close by. The
first day, shortly after sunrise—and surrounded by the
early morning smells of fresh earth and grasslands—he
attached a lead rope to the colt's halter and walked him
around the large corral.

The colt was skittish at first, but soon settled down
and walked at a steady pace behind Ty. After several
turns around the corral, he returned to the pasture.

In the afternoon Ty brought a hand-tooled saddle and
Navajo saddle blanket from the tack room and set them
on one of the corral's heavy wood fence rails. When he
led Trotter back to the corral with the lead rope on his
halter, he stopped beside the saddle and blanket.

Trotter stood motionless. Anticipating.

Ty placed the blanket on the colt's back. He still
didn't move. His ears flipped back then returned forward. Ty patted him. "Good boy."

He lifted the saddle off the rail and held it under
Trotter's nose. Then he stepped to the colt's side and set
it on top of the blanket.

Trotter snorted. Ty patted him and began connecting
and tightening the flank cinch and front cinch. Trotter
resisted and expanded his stomach, which Ty expected,

but the colt stood still. Ty patted him again, then reached for a shorter lead rope from the corral rail and hooked it to the halter, replacing the longer rope. Chico and Scooter stood nearby watching.

"This might be easier than I expected, boy," Ty muttered. He tightened the cinches and took the lead rope in his left hand and reached for the saddle horn. He placed his boot in the stirrup and Trotter began sidestepping away from him. He struggled to get his right leg over the saddle to the right stirrup.

Trotter fought to gain control. His ears flattened back and all hell broke loose! He arched his back and spun skyward, his four hooves leaving the ground at the same time.

Ty's butt lifted off the saddle as his Stetson flew skyward and he careened off the horse toward mother earth. A lightning sharp pain shot through his neck and shoulder the instant he made contact with the ground.

After thirty seconds—or maybe it was thirty minutes—Ty opened his eyes. He lay on his stomach with a mouthful of horse manure and dirt. His head was turned to the side and Chico was licking his face. He tried to get up but the fire-breathing neck pain pinned him to the hard ground. And his head ached. He closed his eyes and waited for it to pass. It didn't.

"Ty?"

He opened his eyes.

Henry Lewis was kneeling at his side. "Ty, don't move. I'm going back to my truck to call the paramedics in Clayton. Don't move."

A short distance away, Trotter stood watching, his

ears pointed forward and the reins touching the ground. With the side of his face pressed against the ground, Ty's eyes made contact with Trotter's. With the hint of a grin, Ty muttered, "We ain't through yet, boy."

THE AMBULANCE DRIVER with Clayton Fire and Rescue keyed the mike. "Dispatch, Med 3491."

"This is Dispatch. Go ahead 3491."

"3491 transporting a male patient, age 37, thrown off a horse, possible head or shoulder injuries, conscious, breathing normally, no visible bleeding. Advise Union County General we'll be there in approximately 15 minutes."

"Dispatch copies. Will do 3491."

IN THE MONTH Alysa Cody had worked at the hospital, the sounds of ambulance and police sirens became familiar. She was making a child's bed in the Pediatric Ward of Union County General Hospital when 3491's siren turned silent as the ambulance approached the edge of the residential area adjacent to the hospital. She glanced out the window as it arrived at the emergency entrance on 4th Avenue.

TWO PARAMEDICS SAT on either side of Ty's gurney in the rear of the ambulance. His head and neck movements were immobilized with a cervical collar. The paramedics had hooked him up to an IV running with normal saline solution.

"Is someone taking care of my horses?" he mumbled.

"Your friend is taking care of the horses and the dogs," one of the paramedics said. "Good thing he drove over to see you."

"Henry?"

"He said to tell you not to worry. Understand he sold you the colt."

"That Trotter is an ornery one," he grunted. "Still needs some work."

The ambulance backed up to the emergency room entrance. Its two rear doors swung open.

Both paramedics jumped to the pavement, one on either side of the gurney, and pulled it from the ambulance. Ty felt the gurney platform spring downward and the four wheels make contact with the ground.

"In here," someone said. The paramedics rolled the gurney in the direction of the voice.

Ty, still immobilized, surveyed the surroundings. He watched ceiling light fixtures and panels fly by. These people were trying to help him, but he was accustomed to being the one in charge. He knew it was nuts, but he wished they'd all go away.

They entered a trauma room and stopped beside an empty gurney. The paramedics and hospital staff transferred him from the ambulance's gurney to the hospital's with precise, deliberate movements and a minimum of conversation.

"Doc Grant is on his way," someone said.

Ty released his grip on the sides of the gurney. He and Doc Grant were occasional players at the monthly poker night in a back room of the Eklund Hotel. He liked and trusted the man.

CHAPTER 6

Gordon Meese parked his Jeep beside the gray metal hanger at Clayton Municipal Airport and walked across the asphalt tarmac to the first stall where clusters of tumbleweeds engulfed the tricycle landing gear of his Cessna Skyhawk. He grabbed a garden rake from the back of the hanger and tore the pesky Russian thistles away from the wheels.

"Goddamn weeds! Wish you'd blow the hell back to where you came from!"

He opened the cabin door and tossed his backpack across his seat to the passenger seat, then walked around the bird for a thorough preflight check. The aircraft was painted white with red trim. Following the mental checklist he had recited hundreds of times before, he completed the exterior and interior inspections of the plane and pulled it out of the hanger with a tow bar attached to the front landing gear. He returned to the cabin, strapped in, and started the engine.

He taxied out and waved to one of the airport crew standing near the fueling area and obtained clearance to runway two-zero for takeoff. A few minutes later he lined the Skyhawk up on the white center stripe and went full throttle. The roar of the engine and acceleration of the propeller filled the cockpit as he held the yoke and rudders steady. At 65 miles per hour, the nose wheel rose from the runway and the bird lifted into the air. Despite its nearly 40 years of age, the hawk sang like the day it rolled off the assembly line in Wichita.

He climbed, turning to a left downwind departure, and eased back on the throttle, levelling off 2,500 feet above the ground. Ahead was Oklahoma State Highway NS1, the north/south black ribbon of asphalt atop the 103rd meridian separating New Mexico from Oklahoma. He flew across NS1, turned left 270 degrees, and headed south along the center of the blacktop, crossing Highway 56 to Feeder Road. To the left, Oklahoma's *No Man's Land*. Straight ahead: Texas.

He adjusted power settings and reset the aircraft trim while two ranch houses and a tall metal silo passed beneath the right wing. The concrete boundary marker he and Ken Lively discovered a few weeks earlier slipped beneath the Skyhawk's nose. With airspeed set at 130 MPH, he continued southbound into Texas and began memorizing landmarks. The next flight would be at night—off the radar—at 500 feet. Today's destination and the nighttime destination: the 103rd meridian at the 32nd parallel. Distance: 260 nautical miles.

In both Texas and New Mexico, Gordon looked down at the abundance of circular agricultural patterns. Patterns created by central pivot irrigation systems spraying water drawn from the depleting Ogallala aquifer on fields of corn, wheat, and alfalfa. Precious water, some of which evaporated before it ever touched the ground. Water drawn from the aquifer by short-sighted farmers in both states. Some of the patterns stretched one or two miles in diameter. A few displayed intricate geometric designs created by mowers and harvesters.

To the right front stood a large metal farm equipment building and beyond it, Texline, Texas—good landmarks to remember for the night flight. Then more circular patterns and, south of Texline, a cattle feedlot with 20 to 30 holding pens. In the distance, beneath his right wing he saw the Daggett Ranch. Ty's red 10 year-old GMC pickup, parked in front of the ranch house, appeared as a small red dot.

Gordon glanced at the aeronautical chart on his lap and placed a check mark at the 36th parallel he now crossed.

His mind drifted to the woman at the Rabbit Ear. Where was she? *Who* was she? It was almost an illusion, the way she appeared out of nowhere—reminding him of Molly. He peered ahead at an empty spot in the cloudless blue sky, picturing the woman walking on the Santa Fe sidewalk.

Without warning, the engine coughed and sputtered. He shot a look at the fuel gauges on the left side of the instrument panel and cursed himself for failing to monitor the left and right fuel tanks.

"For Christ's sake, Meese!" He adjusted the fuel selector valve and returned his attention to piloting the aircraft. The engine quieted down.

Several miles farther he crossed Highway 54, which ran parallel to railroad tracks. To the left, Dalhart, Texas, and a field of pumping units Ken Lively called "nodding donkeys." On the right, Nara Visa, New Mexico, with its near-circular pattern of trees and homes.

He decreased power and descended to 1,000 feet as he approached the Canadian River running east/west from New Mexico to Texas. To the right jutted a bluff with a rock overhang; below it, out of sight, a cave. His hideaway. A cave he discovered years earlier during an overnight campout on an overlook beside the Canadian.

He circled the overhang and rocked the Skyhawk's wings in affectionate greeting, then increased power, climbing back to 2,500 feet.

Ahead lay flat, open desert country and Interstate 40 between Tucumcari and Amarillo. Easy to spot with nighttime freeway traffic. Beyond it, Glen Rio, New Mexico, and the invisible 35th parallel. The Skyhawk held steady at 180 degrees. With little air turbulence, the only sounds were the purring engine and occasional radio chatter from Air Traffic Control.

He crossed over a pronounced east-west stretch of rugged plateaus and bluffs then flat terrain once again. The sole vegetation, mesquite and weeds.

Beyond Jal, New Mexico, the GPS directed him to the destination point, 103/32. He was surprised and dismayed to find what he had suspected: a landscape featureless except for endless acres of oil fields and nodding donkeys. And a maze of crisscrossing dirt roads. Eye-popping oil extraction and recovery operations everywhere... Texas Tea... *You want this land back, New Mexico? Sure, pal!*

The dirt servicing roads offered possible landing sites. He eased back on the throttle and began a circular descent. It would be in the early morning daylight when he arrived on the next flight with the aircraft carrying little weight, only himself and a fifty percent fuel load. He caught sight of two dirt roads close to the target point—roads somewhat isolated and perpendicular to each other. Depending on prevailing winds, either road would provide a satisfactory landing option.

"Hot damn!" He made two low level passes to make certain no overhead power lines or road signs were present; either could catch a wing and turn the aircraft into a Frisbee.

A piece of cake. In a matter of a few hours, Gordon had flown from 18th century cattle country at New Mexico's northeastern corner to 21st century oil country at its southeast corner. He now knew the route. He'd memorized the landmarks. He was prepared for the next flight. At night. He advanced the throttle and banked north to Clayton and home.

SEVERAL MILES SOUTH of Texline, Gordon unbuttoned a shirt pocket and pulled out his cell phone.

Ken Lively, in the middle of a serious breakfast of steak and grits at Granny's Diner, glanced at the Caller ID on his cell phone. "Morning, Sarge."

"Kenneth, what are you up to?"

"Having some breakfast before going out to survey a property line for a customer." Ken picked up a slice of bacon. "How about you?"

"Just flying back from a reconnaissance mission." Texline passed beneath his right wing.

"What do you mean?"

"I identified the location of the true southeast corner of New Mexico. Also found a couple of spots to land," Gordon said.

"You still have that recurring illness, Sarge."

"Don't know what the hell you're talking about." Gordon reached beneath the center of the instrument panel to adjust the throttle.

"I call it your obsessive bewitchment. Man, you never tire of taking on a crusade."

"Hell, nothing's wrong with tackling a cause every now and then," Gordon grinned. "Makes the world a better place to live."

"Maybe so," Ken said, "but sometimes risky. I'll never forget the time, when you were crusading for the legalization of marijuana."

"You have the memory of an elephant, Kenneth."

"You stood up during a speech by one of our U.S. Senators and told him he was full of shit."

"Well, he was, goddamnit." Gordon chuckled. "That was fun, wasn't it?"

"Not when the New Mexico State Police escorted both of us out of Albuquerque's Tingley Coliseum."

"Maybe you have a point." Gordon scanned the area around him for other aircraft. "But you just wait and see, Kenneth, my boy. We are going to call attention to this goddamn boundary error. Big time. I'll keep you posted. Gotta go."

"Be careful, Sarge."

"And don't call me, 'Sarge.'"

Ken Lively chuckled. "You'll always be 'Sarge' to me, Gordon. It's a term of affection, old buddy. I wouldn't be around if you hadn't saved my ass twenty years ago."

"And I'd do it again." Gordon paused. "Signing off."

CHAPTER 7

Something about the red Clayton Fire and Rescue ambulance drew Alysa Cody out of the children's ward and into the hospital hallway leading to the Emergency Room. She didn't stop to question what her instinct was trying to tell her or why the siren on Med Unit 3491 sounded any different than the others. She quickened her pace, ignoring the curious glances from other nurses and hospital staff, as she closed the distance to the Emergency Room.

By the time Alysa entered one of the trauma rooms, two paramedics had already transferred the patient to a hospital gurney. She stood back from the gurney as Dr. Jim Grant, the attending physician, began his examination of the male patient, a tall cowboy whose long frame allowed little room at either end of the gurney.

Alysa stepped closer. It was the rancher from the Rabbit Ear. She held her breath.

"Can you hear me?" Doc Grant leaned over him.

"Yeah."

"What's your name?

"Hell, you know my name, Doc!" the patient growled.

"What's your name?"

"Ty Daggett!"

"How long were you unconscious?"

"A minute or so maybe," he snorted. "I don't carry a stopwatch."

Doc Grant held up three fingers. "How many fingers do you see?"

"Looks like three to me."

Grant took his blood pressure and other vital signs— pulse, eye pupil size, and reaction to light—and made certain there was no blood behind Ty's eardrums. "Got a headache? Ringing in your ears?"

"Nope."

"Sick to your stomach?"

"Nope."

"Why do I wonder if you're telling me the truth?" Doc Grant removed the blood pressure cuff. "What day is it?"

"Thursday." Ty coughed. "Any more questions, Doc?"

Grant ignored the inquiry. He stood and placed the stethoscope around the back of his neck. "Ty, I think you may have experienced severe soft tissue damage. Although a concussion is unlikely, I'm going to run you through X-ray. Just to make sure there are no fractures or other serious injuries. After that we'll conduct neuro- logic and sensory exams."

"What do you mean?"

"Eye exam, hearing, reflexes, balance."

"Whatever you say, Doc." Ty's voice sounded tired and hoarse. He lay still in the gurney, arms at his sides. "Just don't keep me in here too long. I got work to do. I got a ranch to run."

"Like breaking a horse?" Grant pursed his lips.

"Where'd you hear about that?" he rasped.

"Word gets around."

Doc Grant looked up at Alysa standing on the other side of the gurney. "Are you the new nurse?"

"Yes, Doctor."

He reached across the gurney, in the sometimes informal atmosphere of a hospital emergency room. "Jim Grant."

Alysa shook his hand. "I'm Alysa Cody. Pleasure to meet you."

"I've heard good things about you."

"Thank you." She smiled.

"Just moved here from someplace in Texas?"

"Yes, central Texas."

"What brings you to Clayton?"

"A few years ago, my former husband and I purchased a rental property here in hopes of spending time in Clayton during our retirement years. I took a liking to the town. Over time his interests drifted elsewhere."

"I understand." He paused. "Welcome to Clayton."

From the outside came the familiar sound of another med unit approaching. Doc Grant glanced down at Ty, then back at Alysa. "Are you free now?"

"Yes, Doctor."

"I'd like for you and one of the orderlies to take Mr. Daggett to X-ray for upper body film studies." He turned as the ER door opened and called to the EMT. "What do we have?"

"Motor Vehicle Accident. Possible broken leg," the EMT shouted.

He glanced back at Alysa. "Let me know when the X-rays are done."

She nodded to Grant, then motioned to an orderly beside the door. The orderly strode across the room and gripped the end of Ty's gurney and then steered it to X-ray while Alysa walked alongside with the stainless steel IV stand. She looked down. "You doing okay?"

"Yeah," Ty said in a gravelly voice. "You sure look familiar, ma'am."

She smiled and patted his arm.

"And you told Doc Grant your name is Alysa Cody."

"We've not been formally introduced, Mr. Daggett, but I am indebted to you."

As they neared X-ray, the orderly turned the gurney toward the wide entrance.

"How come?" Ty said. "What did I do?"

"We can talk about that later." She patted his arm again. "Right now I have to assist the X-ray technician. We need to get those pictures for Dr. Grant."

"Now I remember." He raised his eyebrows. "You're the lady at the Rabbit Ear Café."

Alysa nodded.

"The lady with the smart-aleck husband."

"The *former* smart-aleck husband, Mr. Daggett."

THE FOLLOWING MORNING, Doc Grant walked into Ty's room. "How you feeling, Ty?"

"Wonderful, Doc. Just wonderful. I really like you and all these other fine people, but I've got work to do. Can you get me outta here?"

Doc Grant sat on the edge of his bed, holding Ty's chart. "After reviewing the results of your neurologic exam and X-rays, I'm confident you *may* have suffered a minor concussion, Ty. Nothing more serious. To err on the side of caution, however, I'm going to ask you to take it easy and stay off that new colt for at least another week."

Grant wrapped a blood pressure cuff around Ty's arm. "If you experience headaches or dizziness, let me know immediately."

"Whatever you say, Doc."

Doc Grant chuckled. "Sure, Ty." He released the cuff. "Blood pressure looks good." He tapped his shoulder. "Take it easy, cowboy. I don't want to see you back here in the emergency room."

HENRY LEWIS WAITED in his Dodge Ram pickup at the hospital entrance. An orderly walked out with Ty and stood by until he was strapped into the passenger seat with the door closed.

Ty thanked him, then turned to Henry. "Did you bring my hat?"

"It's on the back seat."

Ty reached back and retrieved the dusty Stetson and put it on. "You'll never guess who I met here at the hospital."

"I wouldn't have a clue." Henry pulled up to the stop sign at Monroe Street. He peered both ways, then turned left and worked his way across town to Highway 54 and headed south to the Daggett ranch. "Not a clue."

"Remember the lady we saw at the café when we had lunch? When I bought Trotter?" Ty reached up and adjusted his hat. "Her husband was giving her a hard time and we pinned his ears back."

"*You* pinned that pompous jackass's ears back. I just watched." Henry scoffed. "She's a nurse at the hospital?"

"Been there a month. Her name is Alysa Cody."

"Hmm." Henry turned. "Did Alysa take good care of you, Ty?"

"As a matter of fact," Ty's face colored, "she did. She's a good nurse."

"I'm glad to hear that." Henry chuckled. "Don't go getting sweet on her, Ty. That's one tough husband she's got."

Ty looked straight ahead. "He's a horse's ass. Besides, they're getting a divorce."

"Uh-oh." Henry laughed. "Watch yourself, boy!"

THE HOUSE MICHAEL and Alysa Cody had purchased was located off the highway to Des Moines, just outside Clayton. A two-bedroom, yellow brick home sitting on two-and-a-half acres of country property. In a few days the title would transfer to Alysa.

As she drove home in the early evening after a nine-hour shift, she reflected on Ty and his brief stay in the hospital, wondering if he would follow Dr. Grant's orders to take it easy. She had thought of him often since his intervention with Michael, the day he defended her in the restaurant parking lot. Yesterday and today he was just one of several patients in need of her care and comfort, both of which she gladly provided.

Ty Daggett was also a special patient.

She had visited his bedside more often than was required. The tall rugged rancher was an intelligent and independent man. In her mind, a real catch for some fortunate woman. But it was too soon—at least it seemed to be. Too soon after her divorce from Michael to be attracted to another man and too soon after resuming her nursing career.

She learned from Ty's chart that he had no family or next of kin; he was the only child of deceased parents. And he was two years older than she. The person to whom he had given general and medical powers of attorney was "Henry Lewis, local rancher."

As she turned right from the highway into the driveway, a Swainson's hawk rode the wind currents above the grasslands behind her property. She'd seen the hawk on the National Geographic channel on television. In the background, northwest of Apache Canyon, were the purple hues of Rabbit Ear Mountain and the smaller mountain beside it.

She stopped and watched the hawk as he circled, riding the air currents, then she nearly jumped in surprise when he made a lightning dive toward an unsuspecting deer mouse. A split second before he was to become dinner, the mouse shot beneath a large stone and burrowed in. Opportunity lost, the hawk reversed course and flew skyward to circle once again.

In the distance, the sun slipped slowly beneath the horizon and disappeared. She continued down the driveway. An ear scratch and tummy rub for Clemmie, her cat, was first on the agenda, followed by a hot shower and a glass of wine. Then a light dinner and perhaps a TV movie. She reached up to the visor above her head and pressed the garage door opener.

As she waited for the door to go up all the way, she almost laughed at herself. Since when did she come to believe dinner and a movie alone was a perfect evening? What was wrong with her?

CHAPTER 8

As she left the library at Loretto Heights School of Nursing in Denver, Sandra Donovan nearly dropped her stack of books. She didn't know when she'd find time to read another historical novel or biography, but tonight the adventures of Joan of Arc, Bernadette Soubirous, and Mother Teresa held more charm for her than pharmacology or biology. Maybe the classic movie channel would show "The Song of Bernadette" again soon. She thought Jennifer Jones was perfect in the role and had deserved her Oscar for convincing the audience she saw apparitions of the Virgin Mary at Lourdes.

When she arrived at her apartment in Residence Village, Sandra let the books slide to her study desk, and she pulled out the flyer she had picked up at the faculty counselor's office that afternoon.

Would a 100-plus-year-old convent in Baton Rouge accept someone like her? The nuns who arrived from Europe at the turn of the last century had been courageous in their service to the impoverished in that area. Ever since then, their focus was healthcare. Maybe Sandra's degree in nursing would give her the edge she felt she needed. And the chance to pursue her dream.

She turned the flyer over to the back page and noted the address. After graduation, she would apply to the Order and pray to be accepted. If not, perhaps Mother Teresa would find some use for her in Calcutta.

MANY YEARS LATER, Sister Sandra Donovan sat outside the office of Mother Superior Katherine Hebert, waiting for the Mother Superior to complete a telephone conversation with a caregiver in one of the local clinics. She glanced out the window at the darkening sky.

As she waited, Sandra thought of her childhood in rural New Mexico; growing up on the family farm, leaving to become a nurse, considering (and declining) marriage to Ty Daggett. Becoming a religious sister. A religious sister who, during the next several years, would care for the sick and the injured in North Africa and in Louisiana. Along the way the initials "MSN" and CNM" were added behind her name, noting a Master of Science Degree in Nursing and certification as a Nurse Midwife. Of late, the commitment she made years earlier, to life as a bride of Christ, had begun to falter.

After finishing her telephone call, Reverend Mother Katherine stood in the office doorway and smiled down at Sandra. "Come in, Sister. Let's visit."

The Reverend Mother, 20 years Sandra's senior, motioned to one of the two wooden chairs in front of her desk. She sat in the other one. "I apologize for asking you to meet with me so late in the evening, Sister, but it seemed like the only time either of us had free."

"I understand, Reverend Mother."

"I'll get right to the point. I've learned during the last several years to pick up signals from our sisters. Sometimes these signals indicate that their bonds to the order, the Holy Father, to Christ, have begun to soften." She reached across and took Sandra's hand. "And I am sensing that softening in you, Sandra. Am I correct?"

Sandra wore a white cotton blouse and light blue sweater. A navy blue veil rested across her head and down her back, permitting a glimpse above her fore-head of her telltale Donovan red hair. She looked down at their connected hands. "I was young and idealistic when I took my vows, Reverend Mother. The ink on my nursing school diploma was still damp." She smiled an apologetic smile. "In retrospect, I perhaps should have allowed myself more space between becoming a nurse and becoming a postulant."

"That's not unusual, Sandra. It happens to many of us. When we answer the calling, we accept the sacrifices. It is not always easy. And we sometimes have moments of doubt. Because we are human." She withdrew her hand from Sandra's. "Our population of religious sisters has dropped, as you well know. Nationwide—across all orders, nuns *and* religious sisters—our numbers today are a quarter of what they were fifty years ago. We have the fewest number in our community today than I can recall."

She sighed. "I do not want to lose *you*. I think there may be reasons for your wavering dedication. Would you share those reasons with me?" She stood and walked around to the other side of her desk.

Sandra bent her head and put her fingers to her lips.

Then she looked up. "During recent months, Reverend Mother, I have thought about the needs of those at home in the small towns and villages of northern New Mexico. People in need of healthcare and social services we can provide. And I wondered… if the Order might consider transferring me to that area to care for the less fortunate while there is still time."

"Still time for what?"

"Time for me to establish a small clinic. While I'm still relatively young."

The Mother Superior shook her head. "No, Sandra, the Order cannot consider such a request. Absolutely not! We have neither the financial resources nor the personnel to consider such an undertaking."

"Very well." Sandra's hands tensed." I understand."

"Something else is troubling you. What is it?"

Sandra took a deep breath. "During the time I have been a religious sister, I have been where I should have been and doing what I was supposed to do—serving God and the sick and injured in our care."

"But?" The Reverend Mother's jaw tightened.

"But I am not the compliant, starry-eyed, innocent girl who left the ranch in Miami, New Mexico, two decades ago. I am now a grown woman and, I hope, a wiser woman."

"Go on." Her hands were clasped on her desk.

"I am also becoming frustrated by the increasing interference with our efforts to provide healthcare. Politicians and insurance companies demanding to know what we are doing, why we are doing it, and how often we are doing it. My obedience to this absurdity is being tested, Reverend Mother."

"I understand. So is mine. But it is the way things are done today. Such change is God's will."

"Excuse me, Reverend Mother?"

"I said it is God's will."

Sandra's face reddened. "How can you say this is God's will? These people are not healthcare professionals." Her voice cracked. *"We and our doctors are!"*

"I don't believe we are having this conversation. What has become of you?"

"And," Sandra said, "you are saying we must silently and obediently accept this bureaucratic nonsense *because it is God's will*?"

"I object to your attitude, Sandra. And to your erroneous perspective." Mother Katherine's voice rose. "You sound like one of those shouting, rebellious protestors who carry signs on the streets! You should be in a cloistered order where you wouldn't be bombarded by so much nonsense from newspapers and TV!"

"I don't share your level of acceptance, Reverend Mother, or your rationale." Sandra stared at the cracked coffee cup on Katherine's desk with its variety of wooden pencils and ballpoint pens. Her eyes rose. "There is another issue. The world is changing, but the Church is not. *Why not?* I don't think it was God's intention to create a faith, a church, so dominated by males. Males who are expert at restricting our roles and responsibilities as women of the Church. When I was a young, naïve postulant, I embraced all of these things. Today it is more difficult. Am I a rebel? Perhaps I am. Perhaps I'm rebelling against an all-male hierarchy demanding our total obedience while making every effort to keep us women in our place."

Tears welled in Sandra's eyes. She caught her lower lip beneath her teeth.

"What else?" There was a bite in Mother Katherine's voice.

"What do you mean, 'What else'?"

"What else is troubling you that we might discuss? Thus far, Sandra, this conversation has been unproductive. A waste of my time and yours. And you know it! Perhaps it is the stress. We have all been under a terrible workload." She paused. "Was there a man in your life before you became a postulant?"

"What?" Sandra's brow furrowed. She placed her hands on the side arms of the wooden chair and stood. "What does that have to do with anything? Yes, there was a man. That was a long time ago."

"Tell me about him."

"All right... but I am stunned, Reverend Mother. I never expected this line of questioning."

Reverend Mother Katherine rose from her chair. "Tell me about him."

Now they both stood, separated only by the cluttered desk.

"He and I grew up in the same part of New Mexico. We were in Future Farmers of America together and were fond of each other." Sandra inhaled deeply. "I see where you are going with this." She frowned. "And I don't like it."

"I am sorry you don't like it." Mother Katherine leaned forward with both hands on the desk.

Sandra stepped back.

"Would you like to visit your home in Miami for a week or two? To visit these people in your rural communities? To clear your head?"

"No, thank you, Reverend Mother. I see no need for that."

"Is there anything more?"

"There is not."

"You may be excused."

Sandra turned around and strode to the door of Reverend Mother Katherine's office. She reached for the worn brass door knob and turned it, then hesitated. For thirty seconds there was no sound in the office. No movement.

The Reverend Mother remained standing. She waited.

Sandra opened the door and walked out without closing it.

THE REVEREND MOTHER followed the sounds of Sister Sandra's footsteps down the stairway to the entrance on the first floor. When she heard the front door close, she sat at her desk and lowered her head into the palms of her hands.

CHAPTER 9

Whiskey is for drinking; Water is for fighting over.

Anonymous

* * *

Back at the ranch for five days, Ty had, more or less, obeyed Doc Grant's orders. He experienced no symptoms of a minor concussion. Henry rode over one day with a ranch hand to move a few head of Ty's cattle from pasture to grasslands while Ty watched from the red pickup.

Four days after he was discharged from Union County General, Ty drove across the state line to the Circle J Farms just inside Texas to look at a bull he'd seen advertised in a livestock journal. Turned out the bull was a much finer specimen in the journal photograph than in the flesh.

During the return journey to the ranch, he thought of Alysa Cody—as he had off and on since his discharge from the hospital—her dark wavy hair, her smile, her caring nature. Would she like to go to a movie sometime at the Luna Theater in Clayton? Possibly dinner at the Rabbit Ear? Or the Eklund? She'd been a doctor's wife and likely traveled in different circles than his. Maybe it was time she went out with a rancher.

The stretch of highway Ty drove ran close to the New Mexico/Texas state line. He shifted gears and slowed to a stop, then strode a short distance into an open area off the highway. As far as the eye could see, in both Texas and New Mexico, large central irrigation systems sprayed water on lush farmland that was, until recently, as arid as the Daggett ranch. He took off his Stetson, held it at his side, and shook his head in dismay.

Ty returned to the truck and took a back road to the 1,500-acre spur of Daggett Ranch property inside the Texas border. A few head of his Black Angus grazed with three or four strays from Henry's herd.

Ty had programmed the watering system to draw sufficient ground water to maintain one water tank for the small herd, not for irrigation. Pronghorn antelope also dropped by for watering from time to time. He felt he practiced sensible water management and was easily annoyed - sometimes angered - by others' abuse of limited water resources.

He got out and walked among the few head of cattle, found them all healthy, and returned to the truck. The brief stop reminded him of the need to get off his butt. Branding had already been delayed several days and critical tasks needed immediate attention. It was time to saddle Hannibal and get back to work.

IT WAS LATE AFTERNOON when Ty turned off the highway to the narrow Daggett Ranch road. His great-grandfather had laid out the first two ruts of the road when he homesteaded the property in the early 1900s. It was a time when ranchers, pioneers, and homesteaders headed west, first as soldiers and later with families—to till the soil or raise cattle.

The original Daggett spread grew as additional land was added by subsequent generations. His father, an only child like Ty, graded the road with a borrowed tractor and blade in the 1950s. Ty learned how to drive on the road with a stick shift Dodge pickup at the age of thirteen. His dad taught him.

Ty never forgot the time, when he and his dad were coming back home from town. Ty was driving. They were still on the highway when he shifted gears and stepped on the brake instead of the clutch. The Dodge came to a sudden stop, throwing his father against the dash-board. His dad recovered, then slapped him across the face and threw him out of the truck. He walked the nine remaining miles home. Some memories are like cattle brands; they never disappear.

Nonetheless, Ty missed both of his parents and wished they had not been taken from this life twelve years ago.

CHAPTER 10

When Ty left the tack room the following morning with Hannibal's bridle over his shoulder, the two horses were grazing out in the large pasture. He walked across the corral, where Trotter had thrown him the week before, to the wide metal gate to the pasture. He opened the gate and whistled to Hannibal, a hundred yards away.

The horse looked up, but made no effort to come to him.

He whistled again. "Hey, buddy! Hey, Hannibal! We've got work to do! C'mon, boy!"

The horse lifted his head a few inches.

"Hey, Hannibal!"

Still no response.

He walked across the pasture. "What's the matter, buddy."

Hannibal stood in a wide stance, head down and sweating. Trotter nibbled grass close by.

Ty bridled Hannibal and tried to lead him back to the corral. The horse wouldn't budge. "C'mon, boy." He tugged again. Hannibal eventually responded, plodding reluctantly behind him. When they were inside and Ty closed the gate, Hannibal began kicking at his abdomen while sweat glistened on his dark coat.

"I'm going to check your vitals, boy. Something's wrong." He patted him on the shoulder. "May have to call the vet."

Ty heard the sound of Henry's pickup while he walked to the tack room to get the digital rectal thermometer.

Henry came through the outside door of the tack room as Ty retrieved the thermometer from a filing cabinet drawer.

"How you feeling, Ty?" Henry said.

"I'm fine." He slipped the thermometer into a shirt pocket. "But Hannibal isn't doing too well. Haven't figured out what it is. I'm going to take his temperature and check his pulse."

"That's easier with two people," Henry said. "Let me help you."

They left the tack room and walked to Hannibal in the large corral. The horse seemed listless as he stood in a wide stance with his head down.

"Not looking good, Ty," Henry said. "Might be colic."

"That's what I'm thinking." Ty removed Hannibal's bridle and slipped a halter over his head. He handed the lead rope to Henry. "Can you hold him?"

Ty stood beside the rear of the horse, lifted his tail and inserted the thermometer. It beeped after several seconds and he removed it. "A hundred two-and-a-half degrees. Ninety-nine to a hundred one is normal. Damn!"

Henry placed the tips of his fingers behind Hannibal's eye socket and looked at his wristwatch. "Pulse rate is 50. Too high."

Ty shook his head. "I'm going inside to call Doc Reynolds. He's taken care of Hannibal since he was a colt."

Henry took off his hat and wiped his forehead. "Doc Reynolds is up in Wyoming at his daughter's wedding. I talked to him day before yesterday. You'll need to find another vet, Ty."

Ty turned around. "I don't know another local vet. Do you?"

"Well, I do know a damned good one in Shiprock. Her name is Morgan Bluestone. Took good care of our livestock at the Farmington ranch. But her clinic's on the other side of the state."

Ty studied Hannibal. "Maybe I could take him over to Clovis or Tucumcari in the trailer. They've got good vets." He paused. "But I hate to take him that distance in his condition."

"No, you don't want to do that."

"Well, old boy," Ty scratched the horse's ear, "We'll just do the best we can."

Henry reached back to the small leather holster attached to his belt and pulled out his cell phone. "Let me call Morgan. Maybe she can give us some advice. Just so we know we're doing it right."

Ty looked up. "What if she's not around?"

"Only one way to find out." Henry flipped the phone open and punched numbers.

MORGAN BLUESTONE, a member of the Navajo Nation, had been Henry's veterinarian from the time she graduated from Colorado State University College of

Veterinary Medicine and opened her clinic in Shiprock. Henry and his pregnant mare, Rusty, were her first customer and patient. When family circumstances required that Henry and Clara leave Farmington, he dreaded leaving Morgan, a key member of his ranching operation.

"I'M AS CLOSE as a telephone if you are ever in a jam, Henry," she had said.

Now Morgan stood in her office with her phone to her ear, counseling her friend Henry Lewis and Mr. Ty Daggett.

Henry keyed his cell phone to speaker mode so he and Ty could both talk with Morgan and, more importantly, be able to follow her diagnosis and instructions.

"I'M REALLY SORRY I am not there with you, Mr. Daggett," she said as they wound up their conversation and her evaluation. "An onsite diagnosis would be easier and more definitive. I feel certain, as you do, that we are dealing with colic. And," there was a smile in her voice, "you are in capable hands with Henry Lewis."

Henry grinned.

"I see no need for medication. But please follow the steps we talked about: walk Hannibal for a few minutes every other hour; restrict his food so he doesn't overeat; make sure he has easy access to water; if the sweating turns to shaking, cover him with a horse blanket. Following this regimen should, in a few days, restore his health."

"I understand," Ty said. "He's been a good horse, Doc. For lots of years."

"We'll do whatever needs to be done, Mr. Daggett. Call me in the morning between 8:00 and 9:00 and we'll see how Hannibal is doing."

"Yes, ma'am."

Henry took the phone off speaker mode and placed it against his ear. "Doc, I really appreciate your helping us out."

"Glad to be of some assistance, Henry, and I wish I could be there. Your providing the vitals and your own observations helped me tremendously and saved us time."

"You ever thought of moving to Clayton?"

"You are very kind, Henry," she laughed. "I have all I can handle over here. And I know your Clayton vet, Don Reynolds. He's a good veterinarian. I think Hannibal will be okay. Remind Mr. Daggett to call me in the morning."

When Henry turned around, Ty was already leading Hannibal out to the pasture for a walk. Trotter followed close behind, making Ty wonder if somehow the younger animal knew one day in the not too distant future he would become the lead horse at the Daggett Ranch.

CHAPTER 11

Following the retreat of the Western Interior Seaway 100 million years ago – and the disappearance of dinosaurs millions of years later – the earth's surface went through dramatic changes and evolutions. Among the changes were the creation of canyons, caves, and caverns by acidic activity and by violent ocean currents blasting through subsurface limestone.

* * *

Gordon lifted his work boot from the Jeep's accelerator and veered to the right to avoid running over the coyote carcass. It lay between ruts in the rugged terrain east of Logan, not far from the Texas state line. Three black vultures staggered away from the putrid-smelling canid and lurched skyward. They rode the wind currents until Gordon had distanced himself, then they circled back to conclude their meal.

The Jeep's engine roared while he bulldozed through and around the sand, sage, and mesquite in the ruggedly beautiful back country of Quay County toward his hidden sanctuary above the Canadian River. Around him were canyons, draws, gullies, stretches of grassland,

and breathtaking rock formations. The Canadian River changed its complexion as it traversed the region, some sections casually flowing through open plains, others cutting through lava and stone, creating steep canyons.

Gordon's hair had returned to its wild unkempt state since the long-ago visit to Santiago Luna's barbershop. He bore little resemblance to the well-groomed, spit-and-polish soldier he once was. The unruly hair had become part of his character and his identity. He was comfortable with himself. To hell with everybody else.

Two pronghorn antelope shot across the front of the Jeep. Gordon turned his head for a quick glance as their lily-white rear ends disappeared from view. The Jeep bounced along to a round grassy knoll. On the other side stood the ruins of a nineteenth-century Spanish sheep-herder's home. Beyond that, the hideaway.

Gordon, in some ways, had become more and more the loner; at times, almost a hermit. He even admitted it to himself. And he didn't give a damn. He did his own laundry and cooked his own meals. Took care of himself. Still kept the small apartment on Garcia Street in Logan; he'd lived there since his employment with the state land office. He drove to Clayton a couple times a month to take a spin in the Skyhawk or to visit Ken Lively. That was his life.

He hadn't seen the beautiful mystery woman since the chance glimpse of her months before in Santa Fe. Perhaps she lived there. He still hoped to meet her one day. She so reminded him of Molly.

How he wished he had treated Molly more kindly. He couldn't blame her for leaving; for going back to

Kentucky. She had made attempts to save their marriage, but he ignored her pleas. His drinking worsened. During the three years after she left, he wrote to her a couple of times. Sent flowers once. Never a response. He considered telephoning her one time but changed his mind.

The Jeep hit a deep hole, lifting Gordon's butt off the seat. He laughed and let out a few choice words. During his last visit to Clayton, he stashed a recently purchased New Mexico flag, three feet by five feet, in the Skyhawk's aft baggage compartment. Also stashed was a telescoping, twenty-foot aluminum flagpole with a spring-loaded four-leg base and steel arresting rods. Well-built and strong, even in the windswept desert country of New Mexico's southeast corner, the flag could easily fly for as many as sixty days—unless some irate Texan knocked it down sooner.

After planting the flag, Gordon planned to take photos and mail them to newspaper and television outlets with an accompanying piece about "The Great Texas Land Grab."

The rugged Willys Jeep had travelled this primitive road so many times, it could traverse it without Gordon's direction. Rutted roads, washed out roads, roads through sand, even no roads rarely presented a problem. The Jeep and the Skyhawk were Gordon's most trusted mechanical steeds. Today the vehicle carried its usual cargo of supplies, stacked carefully beneath a green canvas tarp.

As he approached the ancient abandoned homestead with crumbling walls of stone and red dirt, a large tumbleweed rolled across the grassland from the left, bounced off the hood of the Jeep, and continued its journey with the wind at its back. Gordon loosened his grip on the steering wheel and slowed to a stop beside the ruins of the one-room building. A modest structure which, more than a century earlier, was a sheepherder's home, his claim of ownership, his dream. A dream likely erased by weather and hard times. Close by were more scattered stones and ruins of what was once a corral for his sheep. Relics of the past.

Gordon turned off the engine and walked to what had been the homestead entrance. He paused for a moment to pay homage to the hardy tenant of that earlier time, standing in the same spot as the tenant stood after laying the stones—hundreds of them—square, round, odd shapes. The footprint of the structure would measure close to 800 square feet. Its walls, once eight or nine feet high, were now two to four feet high. The original rust colored stones were spread about with much of the adobe sealant returned to the earth.

Gordon had checked the records at the county clerk's office. This land and its ruins, located north of Stagecoach Gap, were the property of the State of New Mexico. Prior to the Homestead Act of 1862, the land belonged to no one; there were no boundaries or titles of ownership. In his mind, the land had been there to provide sustenance and comfort to those indigenous Indian tribes and wildlife. But when the Europeans arrived, with their customs and their laws, this changed. The plains, the mountains, and the deserts were divided into territories and states and sections for the

Europeans. For Indian tribes, reservations were created. For wildlife, sanctuaries and preserves. For the buffalo, barbaric slaughter.

He returned to the Jeep and drove down the slope on the back side of the homestead and parked in a concealed spot to the side of a gully. He unloaded a few camping items and extra bottles of water and spread a green and tan camouflage tarp over the Jeep. Then he filled a backpack with the supplies and hiked to the overhang 100 yards upstream in the dry wash. Beneath it, barely visible, lay the opening to the cave.

LATE ONE EVENING, twenty-five years earlier, during the waning days of summer, Gordon sat on the ground behind the overhang with his arms wrapped around his knees. A fiery red sunset glowed to the west. He had driven from Logan to camp out on the sandy grasslands beneath bright stars and the Milky Way. As the sun began to slip out of sight beneath the western horizon, something flew out from beneath the ground a short distance in front of him. At first he thought it was a bird, scared from its nest. Then a second winged creature followed the first. And a third. During the next thirty seconds, dozens of bats flew out.

Gordon pulled a flashlight from his backpack and inspected the rocky terrain in the fading evening light. He spent several minutes navigating across the protruding flagstone ledge until he reached the space below the small overhang. Once there, he pointed the flashlight beam straight ahead and discovered an opening perhaps ten feet wide and three feet in height, created during decades of soil erosion, wind, and rain.

After a few minutes of speculating what might be on the other side of the opening, he opted to postpone further exploration until daylight. He returned to higher ground and rolled out his bedroll, then opened the cans of Vienna sausage and fruit cocktail he'd brought along for dinner. Soon, the Big Dipper and the Milky Way appeared above and he drifted off to sleep.

In the morning he again examined the crevice opening. It appeared to be a tiny cave with a lighted interior. Perhaps a small air vent to a larger cave.

The following spring he had returned with compact geoelectrical detecting instruments he'd used during an earlier geological expedition for the land office. After two days of measurements and scans, using conductive electrodes in the ground, he confirmed his suspicion of an underground void. For the remainder of the summer, as time permitted and without saying anything to anyone, he reconnoitered, explored, and charted his discovery.

The cave, carved out by ocean currents during the waning days of the Western Interior Seaway, was the size of a high school gymnasium. It had smooth walls and, at its highest point, the walls reached nearly thirty feet in height. A second opening overlooked the Canadian River valley, hidden from outside observation by its location within a crevice fold on its face.

Gordon found colonies of several hundred bats clinging to the cave's ceiling. At the back of the cave were layers of guano, replete with its telltale smell of moist air and sulfur. He constructed a primitive scaffolding beneath the original entrance, which allowed him to climb down to the floor of the cave, where he created his own space near its open window above the Canadian River. Here he kept his bedroll and supplies securely stored in Army surplus ammo boxes, safe from weather and inquisitive varmints.

NOW, TWENTY-FIVE years later, Gordon hiked to the cave's hidden access way and worked his way down the scaffolding to the cavern floor. He gazed up at the ceiling where they hung. Hundreds of them. His friends, the bats. Evening approached and that meant time for them to stir. At sunset, they would drop from their roosts and fly out in their random but precise sequence to search for insects.

After a snack of cheese and crackers, he strolled to the large cave opening and stood at its edge. With nothing between him and the Canadian River below except air, he spread his arms and fantasized launching from the ledge and flying down and across the river valley to the other side.

As the sun touched the horizon, the sky turned a deeper red. When half the sun disappeared, the first bat, the scout, dropped from its position and flew outside. A few more followed. Then came a steady stream as the face of the cave slowly changed in color from orange red to gray.

Gordon stepped back from the edge and reached for his backpack while the remaining few bats exited the cave. He pulled a bottle from the brown canvass backpack and took a swallow. Then he took another swallow, bigger this time, and returned to the opening to sit on its edge.

Planets and stars lit up the sky as it darkened into night. Before long, dropping temperatures sent him padding back to his bedroll. And sleep.

CHAPTER 12

Ty's pickup and trailer waited sixth in line at the Five States Auction yard north of Clayton. Chico and Scooter sat on the front seat of the cab with him. Ahead, four more heavy pickups, also pulling trailers, and a semi awaited their turn on the scales. A double-decker trailer, often called a "bull wagon," was behind the semi-tractor. Designed to transport two levels of cattle, the bull wagon held several head of Black Angus steers.

More trucks and trailers were strung out along the side of the highway, waiting to join the caravan inside. All contained nervous livestock, primarily cattle. Some held horses or goats. Several head of livestock were already confined in many of the auction yard pens.

Ty pulled up to the weigh station with three heifers in the trailer. "I hate to do it, Barney," he said to the cowboy at the gate. "You get attached to these cows."

"I hear that a lot, Ty. It's tough to hold on to a heifer that hasn't produced a calf. She doesn't make you any money." Barney, five years younger than Ty, wore the same gray cowboy hat he'd worn at Clayton High School. The hat had character. Word around town was that his parents had bought a new hat for him when he graduated. His wife of two years bought one for him as a wedding present. Both were still in their boxes in his closet.

Barney wrote down the numbers from the scales before and after the heifers were unloaded into one of the holding pens and calculated a quick weight measurement. While Ty and Barney visited, another auction yard cowboy herded the three cows into one of the holding pens.

Ahead of Ty stood the large lath and plaster auction barn with its farm-green-colored walls and corrugated metal roof. Chico and Scooter poked their heads out the passenger window and observed the action while Ty pulled out into the large parking area in front of the barn. He parked between two semis and walked the dogs out to an open field to run around for a few minutes. After they jumped back in the truck, he raised the windows half way, closed the truck door, and continued to the auction barn.

Cattle bawled from the holding pens. A cowboy herding newly arrived livestock to their assigned enclosures whistled to Ty as he approached the side door to the barn. Ty lifted his Stetson and waved back.

After entering the barn and proceeding through a walkway behind the auction arena, Ty walked to the rear of the building and the business office, crowded with buyers and sellers signing in. Three sharply dressed women kept the crowd and their checkbooks moving.

After registering the three heifers, Ty strode across the walkway to a small café where ranchers, cowboys, buyers, and sellers gathered for scrambled eggs and gossip before the 11:00 AM auction.

Henry Lewis sat by himself reading the morning *Union County Leader*. He looked up and waved. After Ty grabbed a plate of scrambled eggs and bacon with a cup of coffee, he pulled up a chair beside Henry. "You buying or selling this morning?"

Henry put the newspaper down. "Just dropping by to see what the market is doing." They shook hands. "And I saw a good looking bull out in the pens on the way in. I might bid on him. What about you?"

"I brought three black heifers in to sell." Ty reached for the salt and pepper shakers and sprinkled the eggs.

"You feeling okay now that you've been out of the hospital a couple of weeks?" Henry stirred some cream in his coffee.

"Yeah, feeling fine. Thanks." Ty picked up his fork and stabbed the eggs. "I'm going to start working Trotter again. Sometime in the next few days."

"Want me to ride over?"

"No, I'll be all right." Ty chuckled. "I've broken a lot of horses, Henry. Some have been easy; some have been more of a challenge. Trotter is a damned good horse. I know him better now." He buttered his toast. "He's a high-spirited colt with a mind of his own. Going to do a couple of things differently this time around." He picked up his coffee cup.

"Good man." Henry glanced up at the round plastic clock on the white wall. "You going in to the auction?"

"Yeah, for a few minutes." Ty emptied his coffee cup. "I'll come with you."

The auction barn was a cavernous place with concrete tiers slanting upwards on two sides and rows of blue fiberglass seats looking down on the viewing pen and the auctioneer platform behind it. There were probably 250-300 seats in all. The scene resembled a family gathering with lots of handshakes and acres of Stetsons, mostly gray, with a few black. The cowboys were solid men with tanned skin and crow's feet at the outer corners of their eyes. Some showed signs of earlier injuries with their limps and reluctant joints.

At 11:20 AM, a few minutes late, the auction began. The first animal brought into the arena was a lively chestnut mare. Bidding started slowly, then quickly hit high gear and took off like a rocket on rails. Ty and Henry stayed with the auctioneer's Mach 1 staccato delivery all the way and agreed with the mare's sale price of 26 dollars a hundred-weight. The horse was led from the arena to a holding pen to await the buyer and his trailer.

Next came two baby goats. "Look at those little critters," Henry said, with a smile breaking on his face. "They're cute as can be with that shiny black hair. Just cute as they can be. They gotta be brother and sister." He nudged Ty. "Bid on 'em!"

"Oh, no," Ty laughed. "I've got all I can handle already. You go ahead."

"I'd like to, but Clara would think I'd gone over the edge if I came home with those little critters in the back of the truck."

Forty-five minutes and several animals later, Ty's three heifers entered the show area. Buyers got a good close-up look at the animals. Behind them, the auctioneer and two assistants sat with computer screens in front of them keeping the auction moving forward. Taped to the sides of the heifers were cards with the numbers 9451, 9449, and 9444.

"Good looking stock," Henry said.

Ty watched the animals and winced at the confusion and fear in their eyes. They were sold at what he considered a fair price. The buyer, a friend of his, was a short fireplug of a man who would likely fatten them up, then ship them off to a stockyard and slaughter.

"Think I'll get back to the ranch." Ty stood and placed a hand on Henry's shoulder.

Henry looked up. "I'm going to stick around a bit longer for that bull. You and Trotter behave yourselves." He grinned. "I'll be thinking of you."

A HALF HOUR LATER Ty entered the Wilson Street lobby entrance of Union County General Hospital and the familiar antiseptic smell of hospitals greeted him. The receptionist, a middle-aged woman wearing a light pink smock, looked up. "May I help you, sir?"

Ty held up a brightly colored bouquet he had stopped to buy at Mary's Flowers on Main Street. "Yes, ma'am, I brought these flowers by for a nurse who helped me out when I was a patient a couple of weeks ago. Her name is Alysa Cody." He cleared his throat and his face turned a shade of pink. "Is she in today?"

The receptionist took an admiring glance at the floral arrangement. "What a lovely thing to do." She smiled and reached for the telephone. "What's your name? I'll find Alysa."

"Ty Daggett." He tipped his hat back. "She might not remember me. I was breaking a horse. Got thrown. She took care of me."

"Have a seat, Mr. Daggett. I'll find Alysa and tell her you're here."

He sat in one of the visitor chairs against the windows in the carpeted area and placed the flower basket on a small table beside it. He glanced at the magazines on the table. Most were baby magazines or maternity publications.

"Ty."

He turned. Alysa Cody walked toward him, smiling and wearing her signature scrubs.

Ty stood. "I brought you some flowers, Alysa. To thank you for putting up with me here in the hospital."

"Why, thank you." She took the basket and held the flowers under her nose.

"I hope you like 'em." He blushed.

"They're heavenly!" She sniffed the bouquet again then leaned upward and kissed him on the cheek.

The receptionist smiled then glanced down at her desk, busying herself shuffling paper.

Ty took off his dusty Stetson and looked down at Alysa. She stood almost a foot shorter. He blushed again. "Thank you."

She smiled. "You're welcome."

He glanced toward the door. "I should probably be going. Chico and Scooter are waiting for me."

"Chico and Scooter?"

"My dogs. They don't like me to be gone too long."

She patted his arm. "I understand. I'm an animal

lover, too."

He put his hat on. "Maybe I can take you to dinner sometime."

This time Alysa blushed. "That would be very nice, Ty."

TY SAUNTERED ACROSS the hospital parking lot a few minutes later with a grin on his face. The last time he'd been kissed after presenting a woman with flowers was when he gave Sandra a corsage at the Clayton High School prom.

He opened the pickup door and Chico and Scooter greeted him with their wagging tails. He slid behind the steering wheel and patted both dogs.

"I think Ty Daggett may have done something right for a change. I hope this one doesn't head for a convent." Then he laughed. Scooter licked him on the face. He inserted the key in the ignition and started the engine.

CHAPTER 13

Morgan Bluestone, the Shiprock veterinarian, spoke on the telephone with Ty every day until she was satisfied Hannibal had fully recovered from his bout with colic. Their final conversation took place a few minutes before Ty walked from the house to the tack room for what Henry Lewis had called *Act Two of the Ty and Trotter Show!*

Ty left the tack room with a saddle and saddle blanket and placed them on the top fence rail of the corral. Hannibal and Trotter grazed alone in the ten-acre pasture beside the ranch's large corral while the other ranch horses roamed freely in the open grasslands adjacent to Henry's property line.

With a halter over his shoulder, Ty walked across the corral to the pasture gate. He approached the horses and checked Hannibal's pulse rate. Then he stepped over to Trotter. He patted him and slipped the halter over his nose, latching it behind his ears. When he lifted his head, Ty attached the lead rope to the halter. The colt was unusually compliant.

"Feeling guilty for sending me to the hospital, boy?" Ty scratched his ear and led him toward the corral and opened the green metal gate. "How about we go a little slower this time?"

Trotter nickered.

After leading the colt around the inside of the corral twice, Ty stopped and held the saddle blanket under his nose. He patted him on the shoulder and placed the blanket on his back.

Trotter's ears shifted position a few times and he let out a snort.

"Easy boy. Easy." Ty picked up the saddle, let the colt sniff it, then set it on the saddle blanket and tightened the cinch, just enough to keep the saddle in place in case the colt tried to shake it off.

Trotter gave it a shot—without success.

Ty tightened the cinch another notch, and they walked around the corral for several minutes with the saddle and blanket firmly in place. He stopped the horse, removed the saddle and saddle blanket, then patted Trotter on the neck. "This was a good workout, boy. We'll try it again before nightfall." He led the horse to the pasture and took off his halter.

The next day, Ty returned to the corral. An early morning scent of dew met him as Hannibal and Trotter watched from the near side of the pasture. Once more, he placed the saddle and saddle blanket on the fence rail and opened the pasture gate.

Hannibal walked toward him, and Trotter followed closely behind. Once they stopped, Ty tossed the end of the lead rope over Trotter's neck and slipped the halter over his head and led him back to the corral. When Hannibal followed them into the corral, Ty grinned. The older horse's presence might help to calm the colt.

Soon the saddle and blanket rested on Trotter's back. Ty tightened the flank cinch and front cinch and placed his left boot in the stirrup and stood—without swinging his right leg over the horse.

Trotter swished his tail to chase away a fly.

Ty patted him. "Good boy." He got down and repeated the procedure on the other side. Again, a pat. He walked the colt around the corral several times, then removed the saddle and halter.

Afterwards, he opened the gate and the horses returned to the pasture. They watched him as he left the corral. Then they headed to the water trough.

In the afternoon, Hannibal chose to remain in the pasture. Ty closed the pasture gate and, feeling pleased with the progress being made, saddled Trotter and introduced him to a new piece of equipment: his bridle. He let him smell it, then he eased the snaffle bit into his mouth. The colt resisted and raised his head several times, refusing to take the strange object between his teeth.

After a few more attempts, Ty succeeded in coaxing him to accept it. When he settled down, Ty slipped the crownpiece behind his ears and connected the throat latch. He led the colt around the corral with the reins five or six times before removing the saddle and bridle.

"We're doing just fine, young fella. Tomorrow we'll saddle up and you'll take me for a ride."

Trotter nickered.

Ty turned and looked him in the eye. "What did that mean?"

From the near side of the pasture, Hannibal watched the exercise, swished his tail, and leaned down for a drink from the long metal water trough.

MIDMORNING THE NEXT DAY, Ty strode across the corral and through the pasture gate. Again he held the bridle over his shoulder. Hannibal and Trotter faced him with their ears pointed forward. He walked up to Hannibal and rubbed his muzzle. "Wish me luck, old boy." Chico and Scooter stood near the gate watching.

He strolled over to Trotter and scratched his ear. "I'm ready, fella. Are you?" He slipped the bridle bit into Trotter's mouth, eased the crownpiece behind his ears, and connected the throat latch. "So far so good..." He patted the colt and led him back to the corral and the waiting saddle and blanket.

A few minutes later, Ty tightened the flank cinch and front cinch and walked the colt to the center of the corral. He stepped to the colt's left side and flashed a grin, remembering what happened at this juncture before. "Trotter, just give us a mild rodeo this time. None of the heavy stuff. Okay?"

He grabbed the saddle horn, placed his boot in the stirrup, and swung his right leg over to the right stirrup. Trotter bowed his neck and took off at a dead run around the inside of the large corral.

He ran without a break until Ty pulled back on the reins. The colt stopped and halfheartedly arched his back. He snorted, began to arch again, and hesitated as Ty pulled back on the reins and dug his boots into his ribs.

Trotter snorted once more. Ty resumed the run.

The young sorrel's coat gleamed with sweat. The day warmed, giving rise to the smells of corral dirt, horse sweat, and Ty's own. He pulled back on the reins and Trotter stopped. Man and horse were tired. Man and horse had reached an understanding.

Ty dismounted and patted Trotter on his neck. "Good work, buddy."

He removed the saddle and saddle blanket and led Trotter toward the pasture where Hannibal stood watching with his head over the top of the metal gate. He opened the gate, slipped off the colt's bridle, and reached into his shirt pocket. His fingers found one of the white sugar cubes he'd placed there during early morning breakfast. He pulled it out and held it under Trotter's nose for a moment. The colt's large pink tongue curled upward and took it. He gave the other sugar cube to Hannibal and patted his muzzle.

A short distance away a lone coyote howled, announcing a kill—likely a rabbit or other small creature. He was soon joined by cries and wails from other members of the pack.

CHAPTER 14

Ty and Alysa sat at adjoining sides of a square wooden table near the front of the Eklund Hotel restaurant and saloon. Their view out the oval windows was of Issac's Hardware store on the other side of Main Street. A weekday evening and still daylight, the tops of the downtown buildings reflected the orange glow of sunset. The waitress, a local woman named Connie, exchanged pleasantries with Ty. He introduced her to Alysa.

"You're the new nurse at the hospital, aren't you?" Connie held her small notepad and pen in front of her, prepared to take their order.

"Yes, I am." Alysa smiled.

"They behaving themselves over there?" Connie was middle-aged, with short curly brown hair.

"They're wonderful. I really like the hospital staff."

"You met Doc Grant yet?"

"We've worked together with several patients."

Another waitress seated a family with four children between them and the ornate wooden bar at the rear of the room. Connie waved to them, then turned back. "He's a tough old bird, isn't he?"

Alysa looked up. "Doctor Grant? I think he is a very

delightful bird."

"Good thing you said that," she hooted. "He's my brother."

"Small towns." Alysa shook her head.

"Has Ty told you about the poker tables in a back room of the hotel?" She pointed her head toward the back of the room.

"No, he hasn't."

"Ty and my brother, Doc Grant, have been known to play a few hands back there every now and then." Connie chuckled and tapped Ty on the shoulder with her pen. "What'll the two of you have to drink?"

Ty grinned as he took off his Stetson and placed it on the seat of one of the two empty captain's chairs. He touched Alysa's wrist. "What would you like?"

Alysa look up from the menu. "Might you have a merlot or a cabernet?"

"We have both."

"I'll have the merlot, thank you."

"How about you, Ty?" Connie tapped him on the shoulder with her ballpoint pen.

"I'll do the merlot as well."

"I'll be back." Connie returned to the bar.

Alysa picked up the menu. "You've obviously eaten here many times, Ty. Do you have any favorites?"

He opened his menu. "Well, I usually listen politely to the specials, then order one of their steaks." He read the entrées. "Anything you'd like to try will probably be fine. They serve a good pasta." She seemed more relaxed than he had ever seen her at the hospital.

"Thanks for asking me to dinner tonight," Alysa said.

"You're welcome. Hope you enjoy it. And I'm glad you're not on call tonight."

At the table beside them sat what appeared to be a father and teenage daughter. He attempted to engage her in conversation. He tried again. The girl was more interested in texting on her smart phone than talking to dad. His smile faded and he stared out the window at the near empty street while she slouched down in her chair and continued to text. Their communication channel was quickly closing. Maybe it had already closed.

Ty gave Alysa a wry smile. "Being a parent is tough these days."

"I imagine it has always been a challenge. And I'll readily admit I'm probably not up to the task."

"Me neither."

"Time has likely passed us by, Mr. Daggett."

He chuckled. "I suspect it has."

She peeked around at the stuffed heads of trophy animals mounted on the saloon walls: buffalo, antelope, bear, deer. "I'll bet there's some history in this room."

"Lots of it." He nodded toward the lengthy polished bar. "A good bit of horse trading and serious drinking has been conducted across that bar over the years. I'm told, if you look closely, you'll even see a couple of bullet holes in the ceiling."

"You're kidding!" Alysa wore her reading glasses, attached to a silver eyeglass chain. She took them off and gazed up at the ceiling. "I think I see one."

Connie arrived with their wine. "Is he telling you about the bullet holes he claims are up there?"

"Are there really bullet holes?"

"It depends on who you you're talkin' to and how many drinks they've had."

"What do you think?" Alysa said.

"There's two directly over the bar. I think one of 'em might be Ty Daggett's." She pulled out her note pad. "What are you two having for dinner?"

Connie took their orders. As she winked at Alysa, she picked up the menus and tapped Ty on the shoulder with them.

He grinned and lifted his wine glass, clinking it against Alysa's. "To a fun evening."

"To a fun evening." She took a sip. "Have you ever been married, Ty?"

He leaned forward and took the stem of the wine glass. "Came close once, but never made it to the preacher."

"Oh, really? Tell me about it." Alysa set her glass on the table.

Ty glanced out at the street for a moment, then turned to Alysa. "I proposed to a girl one time. Shortly before she left for nursing school."

"And?" Alysa said.

"She said she'd really like to marry me but . . ." Ty swirled the wine in his glass and smiled. "She ended up going to a convent."

Alysa lifted her eyebrows. "Probably worked out for the best, Ty. I can't see you married to a nun." She laughed. "What was her name?"

"Sandra Donovan. She came from a cattle ranching family twelve miles the other side of Springer. A little town called Miami. Miami, New Mexico." He took a sip of wine. "Sandra was a nice girl. I hope it all worked out for her."

"And how about your mother and your father? I noticed on your hospital chart that they had both died. Did they pass away when you were young?"

"Yeah." He reached forward and moved the candle at the center of the table. "While I was in the Air Force. Just a few years out of college. Mom and Dad were driving home from Amarillo. Got hit by a freak tornado."

"How sad."

"I drove over to where it happened shortly after their funeral. About halfway between here and Dalhart. What I saw was a stretch of land that looked like someone came in with a giant broom and just swept all the brush and grass right off of it. Wiped almost clean."

Alysa shook her head. "Terrifying."

The smell of barbeque drifted out to the dining area from the kitchen, and Ty smiled when Alysa lifted her nose and inhaled.

He unfolded the paper napkin and placed it on his lap. "You enjoying single life?"

"I enjoy my work at the hospital. And I'm glad to be free of Michael Cody." She stared down at her clasped hands. "Michael became very difficult to live with and to work with. And there were his outside interests."

"Outside interests?"

"Other women. I became a real shrew when I found out what was going on. I'm not proud of that."

"I suspect it was understandable."

"Perhaps. Divorces are rarely one-sided, Ty. Both

sides play a hand. I'm sure I could have been a better wife."

He gave an understanding nod.

"Back to your original question about single life, I am enjoying it." She ran her finger across a bleached spot on the dark placemat. "But there are moments of loneliness." She paused. "I'll get used to it. My cat, Clemmie, is a great companion."

Ty leaned toward her. "Tell me about Clemmie."

Alysa lit up. "Clemmie's my girl. Clemmie is the boss. She rules the house."

"Sounds like a pretty impressive cat."

"She is a long-haired white cat I adopted from the Humane Society in Waco five years ago. A helpless little kitten at the time. Now she's a big spoiled snowball of a cat with a mind of her own. I love her!"

"How did she get the name Clemmie?"

"I named her after Winston Churchill's wife, Clementine, because of her dignity and class."

"I look forward to meeting her."

"Then you shall!" Alysa tapped her glass against Ty's. "Sometime we'll have dinner at my place and we'll include Clemmie."

"I hope she likes me, since I have two dogs."

"I can promise you she will, Ty. Right now she is probably sitting on a pillowed windowsill watching traffic out on the highway, waiting for my headlights to appear in the driveway."

Connie arrived with their ribeye steaks on white oval platters. Ty waited for Alysa to pick up her steak knife.

He hoped she would notice Clemmie wasn't the only one with dignity and class.

CHAPTER 15

After watching the late night news and weather report, where he learned clear skies and moderate temperatures were forecast for the next three days, Gordon turned off the television and stared at the plastic wall clock above the refrigerator. Since dawn he had been drinking straight black coffee. He wouldn't be able to sleep if he'd wanted to.

The drive north, from Logan to the Clayton Municipal Airport and his fully gassed Cessna Skyhawk, would take ninety minutes. He pictured the New Mexico flag and its aluminum flagpole secured in the aircraft baggage compartment. The aeronautical charts were in the pocket of his leather aviator's jacket. Planned takeoff time from Clayton, 3:00 AM. Arrival at the southeast corner of New Mexico, 6:00 AM—daybreak.

He sat at the chrome/Formica kitchen table and followed the second hand in its circular sweep around the face of the clock. When the thin red hand hit the twelve o'clock position, his pulse quickened, and he stood.

"It's midnight, boys and girls," he muttered. "Time to leave."

Gordon reached for his flight jacket draped across the arm of the lonesome living room chair. The venerable jacket, with its World War II 9th Air Force insignia, was a thrift store treasure he had purchased during an engine repair layover in Colorado Springs in 2005. He walked to the apartment door, flipped the light switch off, and headed for the waiting Jeep parked in front.

He drove over the railroad overpass at the edge of town and headed northeast twenty miles to Nara Visa, once a small commercial hub in the Old West. In 1919, the town had boasted eight saloons, three dance halls and a bank. Decades later, railroads and interstate highways bypassed Nara Visa. By 2010, the tiny settlement's census dropped to a population of ninety-two.

When Gordon turned left and drove through the village on Highway 402 toward Clayton, he saw no streetlights or house lights. Continuing north, the headlights boring through darkness, he nodded to the small white postcard Catholic Church outside of town. "Howdy, God. Wish me luck."

Between Nara Visa and Amistad, Gordon pulled off the road to stretch under a bright moon. As he stood in front of the Jeep with his back to a breeze, a small herd of white-faced Hereford cows watched him from the other side of a barbed wire fence. He and the cows stared at each other for a few moments. Then the Herefords resumed their nighttime graze and he climbed back in the Jeep and headed to Clayton, thirty miles ahead.

Gordon drove through Clayton and parked the Jeep close to the airport on the north side of Princeton Street. Airport facilities were shuttered for the night and the airport road was closed. He walked the couple of blocks to the entrance where the two yellow metal gates were chained together and padlocked. The terminal building and hangers were clearly visible in the bright moonlight.

He bent over and stepped through the three-strand wire fence beside the gates and walked the half-mile down the road to the Skyhawk's hanger. Automatic sprinklers sprayed the golf course on the other side of the road from the National Guard Armory. The night-time air smelled of freshly cut grass.

Approaching the dark open hanger and the Skyhawk, he recalled someone telling him of surveillance cameras at different locations on the airport grounds. Why worry? He wasn't doing anything wrong. He looked at his wristwatch. 2:30 AM. A few minutes ahead of schedule. He'd lift off at 2:45 AM instead of 3:00 AM.

He entered the open hanger and pulled the wheel chocks from beneath the tires and dragged them to the side near the hanger's wall. Then he patted the nose of the aircraft. "We're going to have some fun tonight, girl."

Gordon walked around and opened the pilot side door, gave the interior a quick check with his flashlight, removed the control wheel lock, and made sure the ignition switch was off. Then he performed the walk-around inspection of the bird and grabbed a stray tumbleweed from beneath the nose gear. Tossed it to the side of the hanger.

After completing the exterior preflight, he made certain the fuel tanks were full, then pulled the aircraft out of the hanger with the tow bar. He got back into the pilot seat, strapped in, and started the engine.

The bright moonlight illuminated the taxiways and runway. "The gods are with us, Skyhawk." Five clicks on his mike button would turn on the runway lights, but there was no need to. Mr. Man in the Moon was doing just fine. And, why call unneeded attention to the flight?

He checked the windsock and estimated wind direction and velocity, then lined up at the end of runway zero-two, heading 20 degrees. Other than a few random vehicles on the highway west of the airfield, there were no other signs of life. Time: 2:47 AM. He performed a quick review of the instrument panel and released the brakes, then advanced the throttle to full position and held his heading down the moonlit center stripe.

The exhilaration of the moment quickened Gordon's heartbeat and wrapped his torso and arms in goose bumps. He glanced down at the airspeed as the front gear lifted from the runway. 63 miles per hour. Airborne.

"Hot Damn! Texas, here we come!"

The Cessna eased left, climbing to 500 feet above the ground and crossing Oklahoma State Highway NS1, the same route he followed on the daytime practice run. Gordon turned 270 degrees left and lined up on NS1—heading south, one-eight-zero degrees.

The black asphalt highway beneath the nose of the aircraft turned to a dirt road at Highway 56 and continued to the Texas state line and the boundary monument he and Ken discovered during the Great Tumbleweed Migration. In the bright light of the moon, he caught a glimpse of the monument just as the aircraft entered wide-open country. With moonlight, reliable navigation instruments, and common sense to guide them, he and the Skyhawk were on their way.

Three hours south, sunlight and the objective

awaited them.

He maintained the 180 degrees heading atop the invisible 103rd meridian. Only a few lights on the ground were visible from scattered farms and ranches. Gordon spread the aeronautical chart across his lap. To avoid the brightness of a standard flashlight and its impact on his night vision, he turned on his red LED flashlight.

Ahead to the right glimmered the lights of Texline; Dalhart was next on the left. Gordon crossed the invisible 36th parallel. Flight altitude held steady at 500 feet above the ground.

He grinned and patted the yoke. During the next three hours, a few residents of the great state of Texas might be awakened from their deep sleep, he thought. He chuckled as he buzzed a large ranch property with several out buildings and a brightly illuminated equipment yard.

Nara Visa passed to the right. A few miles farther, his hideaway cave. The lights of Tucumcari followed, then Interstate 40 between Tucumcari and Amarillo.

The Skyhawk held steady. Air turbulence was minimal and the balance of fuel between the two tanks stayed even. As was the case during the daylight test flight, the only sounds in the cabin came from the humming single engine and radio communications from other aircraft and Air Traffic Control. He glanced at the chart and noted his flight path passing from Albuquerque Center to Fort Worth Center. Would he be on anyone's radar at this altitude? Hard to tell, but probably not.

As early morning light began to reveal more ground features, he recognized the area near Bronco, Texas, about an hour from the destination. The New Mexico flag and aluminum flagpole waited in the baggage compartment.

Two miles ahead and east of the New Mexico state line, he saw a two-story ranch house with several wood-frame out buildings. He lowered the nose and increased power. Someone with a flashlight scampered from one of the out buildings and entered an outhouse several yards behind it.

At 300 feet above the ground he leveled off and held airspeed at 125 miles per hour until he flew directly over the outhouse with a roar. "Whee! If you folks weren't runnin' before, you sure as hell are now!"

Gordon maintained heading and airspeed for another sixty seconds, hoping to disappear from the rancher's sight. Then he climbed back to altitude and resumed normal airspeed. After a few moments he entered the destination coordinates, 103/32, in the portable GPS unit and attached it to its holder above the instrument panel. Aircraft heading was adjusted one degree left.

"Aircraft flying low level southbound just east of Hobbs, New Mexico, this is Fort Worth Center. Please identify yourself."

Startled out of his reverie, Gordon sat upright and looked around for another aircraft in his vicinity.

"Aircraft flying southbound along the 103rd meridian in Texas at approximately 500 feet, east of Eunice, New Mexico, this is Fort Worth Center. Identify yourself."

"Holy crap! That's me," Gordon muttered. "Must have pissed off a few folks back there." He reached for the mike. "Fort Worth Center, this is Cessna 5877 flying southbound near Eunice."

"5877, did you file a flight plan?"

"5877, negative. Flying VFR, Visual Flight Rules."

"One of our FAA aircraft has had you under surveillance, 5877. You've been doing some pretty risky flying. What is your home base?"

Gordon shook his head. "Shit!"

"5877. Fort Worth Center. What is your home base?"

He keyed the mike. "5877 home base is Clayton, New Mexico."

"Purpose of your flight this morning?"

"5877 flying for pleasure."

"Destination?"

"Southeast corner of New Mexico."

"Say again, 5877."

"Destination is a small dirt strip at southeast corner of New Mexico, then return to Clayton."

"Roger 5877. Contact Albuquerque Center, frequency 127.85 when you return to Clayton. Do you understand?"

"5877 understands. One-two-seven-point-eight-five."

It was 5:56 AM. Gordon knew he'd been doing some pretty crazy stuff. Just didn't think he'd get caught. His heart rate quickened and his hands started to shake.

He glanced at the GPS as the sun began to peek over the eastern horizon. He was closing on the 103rd meridian, 32nd parallel. Ahead was the narrow dirt road he'd identified on the previous visit.

He relaxed for a moment and picked out a touchdown point and circled back around to line up for landing. He began reducing power when he noticed movement from the left side of the road. An oilfield truck barreled down a road perpendicular to his landing strip, on a collision course with his Cessna.

"Holy crap!" He cranked the throttle to full power and lifted the nose of the bird, clearing the surface of the road by no more than ten feet. "Jesus Christ!"

The truck's driver, going like a bat out of hell, never saw him. It disappeared to his right.

Regaining altitude, he circled once again, looking for other signs of life. There were none. Sweat bathed his face and soaked his shirt as he came around and lined up once more. As he descended to touchdown, Gordon's hands began shaking once again.

He inhaled deeply, pulled himself together, and guided the aircraft to a smooth dirt landing, rolling 200 yards to a stop. Sweat dripped from his forehead as he reached to his left and cut the engine. His eyes stung from drops of the salty sweat; he pulled a handkerchief from his back pocket and wiped his eyes then tore off his leather flight jacket and tossed it on the passenger seat and grabbed the GPS unit.

Gordon stepped to the ground and retrieved the canvas shoulder bag containing the New Mexico flag and flag pole from the baggage compartment, then he grabbed the small sledge hammer and holster and hooked it to his belt. It felt like his ammo belt during Desert Storm. The belt that holstered his .45. The surrounding sandy terrain reminded him of the area near Hafar Al-Batin. His hand shook as he held the GPS, and followed its directions to 103/32, 25 yards to his right, midway between two dormant oil derricks.

Gordon dropped the equipment and pinpointed the

spot as closely as he could, drawing an "X" in the arid ground with the side of his boot. He placed his hands on his knees to catch his breath. He thought he heard mortar fire; shook his head and took another deep breath. Then he reached down and opened the large canvas bag.

His hands were still unsteady while he lined up the five flagpole sections. When assembly was completed, he unfolded the three-foot by five-foot New Mexico flag and attached it to the top with stainless steel clips and swivel rings. At the other end was welded a spring-loaded four-leg base. He removed the four steel arresting rods taped to the base and set them to the side, then lifted the flag end of the pole and rotated it to its twenty-foot vertical position and kicked a lever, shooting out the four legs.

Winds were light as is typical during the early morning hours in the high desert. With the small sledgehammer, he drove the four arresting rods into the ground, anchoring the end of each flagpole leg.

He stepped back and looked up at the New Mexico flag—a red sun symbol on a field of yellow. "You are one beautiful flag! Yes sir, one beautiful flag!" His hands stopped shaking and he snapped a salute.

The sun had risen above the horizon, bathing the land in early morning light. The only signs of life were contrails directly overhead, streaming behind a high altitude jet. He reached into a side pocket of the canvas bag, lifted out a camera, and snapped photos of the flag and its surroundings, taking several shots from different vantage points. He hoped the flag would remain flying in the wind and weather for sixty days or more; unless someone from the oilfield or local sheriff's office removed it sooner. In the meantime the photos and The Great Texas Land Grab article would be sent to newspapers and television stations.

He returned to the Skyhawk and patted the nose of the prop. Then he walked around to the cabin to release the brakes and, with the tow bar, pulled the plane around 180 degrees, facing the strip of dirt road he'd landed on several minutes earlier. He tossed the canvas bag and sledgehammer into the baggage compartment, and returned to the cockpit, buckling in, and hitting the ignition.

Takeoff down the narrow oil field road, with scattered equipment on both sides, required all of his flying skills as well as maximum power and forgiveness from the Skyhawk. Once he was airborne he circled back around, rocked the wings, and banked north to Clayton.

During much of the return flight, his mind dwelled on the ass chewing from Fort Worth Center and the consequences awaiting him in Clayton. A few miles south of Clayton and Texline, he took his cell phone from his shirt pocket and called Ken Lively.

"Kenneth, my boy, what are you up to?" Gordon had one hand on the yoke and the other on the cell phone.

"Doing a survey for a title dispute. Just located a pin hidden under some brush." Ken paused. "Are you at home?"

"No, I'm up in the air. I just planted the flag down in the southeast corner."

"By God! Congratulations, Sarge!"

"Thanks." Gordon continued scanning the instrument panel and the sky around him for other aircraft.

"You sound tired. Are you okay?"

"Yeah," Gordon said. "Got the shakes for a little while." He paused. "Bad memories of Desert Storm. But, I'm okay now."

"How long ago did you plant the flag?"

"About 6:00 AM Mountain Time. Right after sunrise. And I'm in deep shit."

"What do you mean?"

"The FAA is on my ass for waking up a few Texas ranchers… and scaring their livestock."

"Uh-oh."

"I'll bring you up to date later."

"Give me a call when you land, Sarge."

"10-4."

Gordon lowered the throttle setting to begin a slow descent. Clayton Municipal Airport stretched to the left of the Skyhawk's nose. He was eager to land and complete the flight. Runway zero-two-zero was in sight. But he didn't look forward to an ass-chewing from Traffic Control. He continued descending.

What would they do? What *could* they do? They can, by God, take away my license and ground my pitiful ass, he thought.

Gordon lowered the flaps. Objects on the ground flew by at quickening speed. He pulled back on the yoke and tapped the right rudder pedal. The asphalt runway rose to meet him. He felt the familiar bump of the landing gear making contact.

They can ground my ass. Shit!

CHAPTER 16

Gordon landed at Clayton Municipal at 10:30 AM and taxied to the fuel area. With no immediate flights in mind, he filled the Skyhawk tanks only half full and continued to the hanger to secure the aircraft. Leaning over the left landing gear, he returned the chocks beneath the tires.

"Gordon?"

He straightened up and turned around.

Ernie Valdez, the airport manager, stood beside the Skyhawk's wing with his hands in his pockets. "Albuquerque Center is looking for you. They want you to call them."

Gordon shook his head. "Yeah, I know." He reached inside the cockpit for his jacket, then locked the cabin door. "I was hoping they'd forget."

"You look whipped. Did you hit weather up there?"

"No, I just didn't get much sleep last night." Gordon ran his fingers through his hair.

"Humph... I saw your Jeep parked out there on Princeton when I came to work this morning and then I saw you on the surveillance cameras when you walked to the hanger. You shouldn't take off in the middle of the night. And with no lights!" Ernie threw his hands in the air. "*¡Qué pendejo!* That's crazy, Gordon."

Gordon said nothing as he walked to the front of the plane and slipped a red canvas cover over the pitot tube.

"Albuquerque sounded pissed. Fort Worth Center called 'em. What were you doing out there anyway?"

"I buzzed a couple places. Scared shit of a Texan running to an outhouse. Literally!" Gordon chuckled. "You got anything to drink, Ernie?"

"At this time of day? Here?" Ernie frowned. "Hell no!"

"Just kidding."

"Albuquerque Center said you should contact them on the radio or by phone. Come on in. You can use my office."

They walked to the terminal and Ernie motioned to the desk in his office. "Go ahead and call 'em." He pulled a slip of paper from a shirt pocket. "Here's the number. I've got work to do at the front counter."

Several minutes later, with his head down and hands in his pockets, Gordon left Ernie's office and walked down the hallway to the terminal lobby. The building was almost empty. One pilot was at a small corner desk, preparing a flight plan for a run to Cheyenne, while a mechanic researched an electronics problem in one of the facility's tech manuals.

Ernie stood behind the counter, leaning over a spreadsheet of arrivals and departures for the past week. He glanced up. "What happened with Albuquerque Center?"

Gordon hunched over the other side with clasped hands and his elbows on the counter. "They chewed my ass out." He glanced down at a grease spot on the counter. "Seems a couple of people phoned in complaints about me disturbing the peace. The bastards."

"Maybe you were, *hombre*. What are they gonna do?"

"They're placing the complaints in my file along with Fort Worth Center's report. If I screw up again, FAA will pull my pilot's license. They're a bunch of assholes."

"Jesus, that's pretty heavy." Ernie stood. "What the hell were you doing over in Texas last night anyway?"

Gordon reached for one of the regional aeronautical charts at the end of the counter and spread it out. "Have you ever heard about the three-mile strip of land along New Mexico's eastern boundary that Texas stole from us?"

"Yeah, I remember my grandfather used to talk about it."

Gordon pulled a felt tip pen out of his shirt pocket and drew a dotted black line down the 103rd meridian from the 37th parallel atop the Oklahoma panhandle to the 32nd parallel. "This line is the eastern boundary Congress established for New Mexico back in 1850. And this, my friend, Ernie," he drew a solid line down New Mexico/Texas state line, "is today's boundary next to Texas—two and a half to three miles west of where it should be."

"Uh-huh."

"In 1859 Texas stole more than 600,000 acres of land from New Mexico. Surveying error, they call it. Despite repeated requests to correct the error, the *Tejanos* have ignored it. New Mexico lacks the political will and financial resources to wage a legal battle against its powerful eastern neighbor."

"You sound like that guy, Don Quixote." Ernie grinned. "Okay, so what were you doing last night?"

"I flew down and erected a New Mexico flag right here! Just inside the west Texas boundary, east of Jal and Lea County" He drew a circle around 103/32. "I took pictures of the flag that I'm sending out to newspapers and television stations in New Mexico and Texas with the story."

"Gordon, you're nuts!" Ernie shook his head and leaned back over the spreadsheet. "Retirement isn't good for you. You got too much free time on your hands."

"Thanks for your support, *cabron*." He rolled up the aeronautical chart and tapped Ernie on the head.

Ernie scratched his chin. "You driving back to Logan now?"

"I'm too tired to drive home." Gordon yawned. "I'll check into that motel on 1st Street, near the Wild Horse Grill, and drive back home tomorrow."

"Want me to drive you out to where you parked the Jeep on the road?"

"No, thanks. I've got some thinking to do. I think better when I'm walking."

ON THE WAY to the motel, Gordon stopped at a liquor store and bought a fifth of Jack Daniel's. He checked in at the motel shortly after noon and poured himself a drink.

At 6:00 PM he woke up fuzzy headed and hungry. A rerun of "I Love Lucy" played on the TV. The bourbon bottle beside the bed was about two-thirds full.

He walked to the sink and splashed water on his unshaven face, then ran a comb through his hair, and drove down the street to the Western Grill.

Several other customers were dining in the restaurant when he walked in and sat at a table near the center of the dining area.

"What would you like to drink?" the waitress said.

"Bourbon on the rocks."

"I'm sorry, sir, we don't serve alcoholic beverages. I can serve you water or iced tea."

He looked at her with glassy, surprised eyes. "You're kidding me, right?"

She smiled. "No, sir."

"Where can a man get a drink with his dinner here in town?"

"Sir, I believe the Eklund Hotel serves drinks with their meals."

He pushed his chair back and stood, balancing himself on the back of the chair, then turned and left.

GORDON ENTERED the Eklund Saloon and Dining Room from the hotel lobby and was escorted to a table near the old ornate bar. Charlie, the heavyset bartender, leaned over the bar, talking with four patrons standing on the other side. They looked like locals. A large buffalo head peered down at him from his left.

Most of the tables were filled with a mix of cowboys, ranchers, and tourists. A color television set mounted high in one of the front corners was broadcasting a quiz program. Four people at the table in front of the set were the only ones watching it.

Connie, the waitress, approached Gordon's table from the bar area. "What'll you have to drink, sir?"

"Bourbon on the rocks." He picked up the menu and studied it for a moment, then put it back on the table. He got up and walked to the men's room behind the bar. When he returned, he downed the drink that awaited him and glanced around the dining room. Didn't see anyone he recognized. Ten minutes later he ordered a second drink and a chicken fried steak.

Half way through dinner, he cut a bite-size piece of steak and put it in his mouth—and he froze. Seated on the far side of the dining area near one of the front windows was the gorgeous woman from the Rabbit Ear. The same woman he saw in Santa Fe.

"Lady, you look so much like Molly," he said to himself. He put his fork down and rubbed his eyes.

Connie approached his table from the bar area. "Is everything all right, sir?"

"Yes, everything's fine." Gordon picked up the empty glass. "Guess I was talking to myself. I'll… take another one of these." His tongue had grown heavier.

She took the glass. "Are you driving tonight, sir?" She studied his eyes.

"No… I'm walking." He wiped his mouth. He knew he was lying, but he didn't care. "This will be my last one."

She hesitated for a few seconds, then walked back to the bar.

Gordon wiped his mouth with his napkin and stabbed a French fry on his plate. He lifted the fork to his mouth and returned his gaze to the woman next to the front window.

She and the man appeared to be in a serious conversation. She faced Gordon as she spoke to the man.

Gordon squinted his eyes. The man was Ty Daggett!

Gordon returned the fork on his plate and stood. He walked toward the men's room, glancing over his shoulder at Ty and the lady just before entering the narrow, dimly lighted hallway. Standing at an adjacent urinal in the men's room was a cowboy who had also had a few drinks. They spent the next several minutes telling jokes to each other.

Still laughing, Gordon walked back to his table as Connie placed a fresh drink at the corner of his place mat. "This is your last one, sir."

"Yes, dear." He winked at her and noticed the bartender observing him as he sat down. He belched and fumbled with his knife to cut another piece of steak. The steak had turned cold. When he finished chewing, he set down the knife and fork and stared at the candle in the center of the table.

AT THE FRONT of the dining room, beside the window, Alysa placed her hand on Ty's wrist. "This has been a delightful dinner, Ty. I've truly enjoyed our second date."

He smiled. "So have I, Alysa." He looked outside. It had become dark. The Isaacs Hardware sign across the street was brightly lit. "We should probably be going. You have an early morning shift at the hospital and I've got ranch chores that need tending to."

She folded her napkin and placed it on the table. "I agree."

As Alysa and Ty approached Gordon's table on their way to the door, Ty stopped. "Hey, Gordon, I want you to meet a friend of mine."

Gordon took his attention away from the table candle and looked up. "Ty!" He stood to shake Ty's hand. Then he turned to the gorgeous woman from Rabbit Ear.

"This is Alysa Cody," Ty said. "Alysa, this is my friend, Gordon Meese."

Tongue-tied, Gordon shifted his weight from one foot to the other.

"Alysa moved here from central Texas recently. She's a nurse over at the hospital."

Gordon held out his hand to Alysa.

She took it. "I'm pleased to meet you, Mr. Meese."

"The pleasure is mine, ma'am." Gordon nodded. Her eyes were brown, just like Molly's. She had a warm smile. "The pleasure is mine."

"Thank you," she said.

"And you are in good company with my friend, Ty Daggett."

Ty took Alysa's arm and patted Gordon on the shoulder. "Take care of yourself, pardner."

"I will. Thanks." He sat down.

Charlie the bartender waved to Ty as he and Alysa walked out the door.

Up close, Alysa was beautiful. More beautiful than he expected. Gordon lifted the glass of bourbon to his lips. But she wasn't Molly. There was only one Molly.

A few minutes later, someone placed a hand on Gordon's shoulder. He looked up. It was Charlie. He had a kindly face. It was also a no nonsense face. "Need any help, buddy?" he said.

"No, I'm okay." Gordon glanced around the dining room. Customers occupied three other tables.

Charlie set Gordon's bill on the table. "I'll be the cashier."

Gordon reached to his back pocket for his wallet and handed it to Charlie.

"No, sir, I'd rather not handle it that way." Charlie looked at the bill. "The amount you owe for three drinks and dinner is thirty-four dollars and eighteen cents. Plus a gratuity for the waitress if you would like to leave one."

Gordon frowned. "How much is that?"

"The tip?"

"Yeah... No, I mean all of it. The total."

Charlie glanced at the bill. "You can round it off at forty dollars. That includes a fifteen percent tip."

Gordon studied the currency in his wallet and pulled out three twenty-dollar bills.

"You gave me one too many." Charlie handed Gordon one of the twenties. "Thank you, sir. Now I'll walk outside with you if you'd like."

He shook his head. "I don't need help."

GORDON WOKE UP the next morning in his motel room with cotton in his mouth and a splitting headache. He went to the bathroom, then back to bed for another hour, then he got up again and managed to brew some coffee. He got dressed and went outside. The Jeep wasn't parked in any of the spaces near his room.

"Aw, shit." He rubbed his bloodshot eyes. It didn't take long before he found it parked in the motel flower-bed, wedged between two spruce trees.

His stomach turned. He wanted to go back and crawl beneath the covers and never come out. The last thing he remembered from the night before was Ty Daggett introducing him to Alysa Cody. He also had a fuzzy recollection of having a few drinks with the restroom cowboy at another bar down the street from the Eklund Saloon.

The Jeep didn't appear to be damaged. Two of the tires bore marks of running against curbs. He got in and started the engine. It sounded okay. He backed out of the flowerbed, broke a few tree branches, and parked in front of a motel unit far from his own.

Gordon gathered his things from the room and walked to the front desk in the motel lobby. The clerk, a grandmotherly type with white hair and glasses, pulled up his registration on the computer screen. "Was every-thing satisfactory, Mr. Meese?"

"Yes, ma'am." He avoided her eyes.

"Just sign here." She pushed the credit card bill across the counter.

"Ma'am…"

"Yes."

"I ran into the flowerbed with my Jeep last night. By accident. You might want to add something to the bill for any damage."

She laughed. "People do that all the time. Especially in the winter when it's under snow." She handed him a pen. "Just sign on the bottom line. Where I marked the 'X.'"

Gordon signed the credit card bill and handed it to her. "That is very charitable of you, ma'am. Thank you."

She gave him a warm, genuine smile. "You're welcome, Mr. Meese. Come back and see us."

He left the motel lobby and walked to the Jeep. His head wasn't down. Nor was it held high. His feelings were a mixture of hangover guilt and gratitude to a kind woman for her gentle forgiveness.

CHAPTER 17

While Gordon Meese was leaving the Eklund Saloon, Ty Daggett was driving his pickup down Alysa Cody's driveway with Alysa at his side.

"A very delightful evening, Ty," Alysa said when Ty stopped the pickup in front of her garage door. "Thank you." She reached for the door handle.

"I'll get it, Alysa."

Ty walked around and opened the passenger door. The smell of early fall was in the air.

"Your mother certainly taught you some manners, Ty Daggett. I don't remember the last time someone opened a car door for me." She laughed. "I mean a truck door."

He grinned as he took her arm. "Mom sure tried. Some of her teaching worked. Some didn't."

Alysa took the house keys out of her pocket and opened the front door then turned, just inches from Ty's face. "Can you come in?"

"Sure. But not for long." He tipped his hat back.

"Why is that?" she teased, as she flipped a light switch to turn on the living room lights.

"I don't like staying away from the ranch too long. And Chico and Scooter are probably sitting on the porch waiting for me."

"I want you to come in and meet Clemmie. Miss Clementine."

Clemmie jumped down from the windowsill and trotted across the room to rub against Alysa's leg. She picked her up and held her. "Clemmie, meet Ty."

Ty reached out and scratched the top of the cat's head.

Alysa closed the door and motioned toward the sofa. "Have a seat and I'll pour us some wine. Cabernet okay?"

As he nodded, a clock in the kitchen chimed nine times. Ty tilted his head and grinned. "I like the sound of that gong."

"It's an antique wooden wall clock. I purchased it in Germany during a European trip with Michael to celebrate our fifth wedding anniversary."

Ty remained standing as he looked around the living room and adjoining dining area. Among the framed pieces on the walls hung photographs of different European locales. Photographs apparently taken on the same trip: Big Ben, the iconic London clock tower; the Acropolis of Athens; Notre Dame Cathedral in Paris.

He sensed simplicity and comfort in the home— with a touch of style. The furniture and gray/tan carpet were high-end department store, but not ostentatious. Comfortable surroundings for what would have been two people in their get-away home. Prior to Michael Cody's exit.

He was admiring the photograph of Notre Dame when Alysa returned from the kitchen with two glasses of cabernet. She handed him one of the glasses, then pointed to the photo. "My favorite cathedral. I'm not

Catholic, but Notre Dame totally takes my breath away."

Ty studied the photo and nodded.

Alysa stepped forward to stand next to him. "Are you Catholic?"

"My mother was. I'm not attached to any organized religion."

"Oh, really? You have no belief system?"

He turned from the photo. "I believe what goes around comes around. During our lifetimes, we each suffer for our wrongs, one way or another. We're sometimes rewarded for our rights."

Alysa looked up and smiled. "And?"

"And, in the end most of us receive a passing grade on to the next life—whatever or wherever that might be."

She tapped Ty's glass with hers. "I don't know as I could disagree with that." She leaned forward and kissed him on the lips.

He returned the kiss and knew the dogs would have to wait.

FOUR BELLS CHIMED from the German clock in the kitchen. Ty opened his eyes. He lay on his back looking up at a ceiling he didn't recognize at first. The only light came from nightlights in the bathroom and the hallway. His right arm curled around Alysa, while her head rested against his shoulder.

Her hair felt soft against his neck as she breathed. He needed to get back to the ranch where days begin at five o'clock in the morning. And Alysa was on the seven o'clock shift at the hospital. He moved his right arm ever so gently.

"What time is it?" Alysa murmured. She placed her hand on his stomach.

Ty turned his head until his lips met her forehead. "Four o'clock. I need to get going. A lot of critters at the ranch will be looking for me real soon. But you stay here and get some more sleep."

He eased out of bed, gathered his clothes, and tip-toed into the bathroom. Five minutes later he returned and bent over her. She lay on her side and her eyes were closed. He kissed the pink birthmark on her neck.

When the front door shut and the truck engine start-ed, Alysa rolled over and buried her face in Ty's pillow.

After a few moments, she turned over and sat on the edge of the bed, then slipped her feet into fuzzy pink slippers and reached for the long-sleeved robe on the bedside chair. She ambled from the bedroom to the kitchen and turned on the coffee pot and walked back down the hallway to the bathroom.

Noticing the soapy water splashed on the counter and mirror, Alysa smiled. "Men!"

She studied herself in the mirror. "Last night was fun, young lady. It's about time, isn't it?" She reached out and turned on the warm water.

SHORTLY AFTER HE turned off the highway to the narrow dirt Daggett Ranch road, Ty drove over a cattle guard and glimpsed at the passenger seat, remembering the image of Alysa seated beside him a few hours earlier.

It was still dark with just a hint of light on the eastern horizon.

He missed Alysa already. But they were from different worlds—she a city girl, accustomed to having people around her or in her care—he, a solitary man of cattle ranching and the soil, happier being surrounded by horses and cattle than by people.

"Take your time, boy," he said aloud as he drove over a second cattle guard. "Take your time."

Golden orange reflections gleamed from the eyes of Black Angus cattle grazing close to the road while they stood watching the truck pass by. Closer to the ranch house, Ty circled by Hannibal and Trotter and the other horses. They lifted their heads as he passed.

When he crested the rise just west of the house, he sensed a foreboding. Chico and Scooter usually ran out from the house to greet him. They were nowhere in sight. Neither of them.

He continued to the house and turned off the engine and headlights. Visibility had increased with the early morning light. When he stepped from the truck, a movement a short distance behind the house caught his attention.

Coyotes! Three of them dashed away as he ran to the rear of the house. His heart sank as Chico limped to him with blood smeared on his white tuxedo chest. Nearby lay Scooter's remains and pieces of her tan fur.

Ty knelt to examine Chico and found a gash on the collie's rear leg, and a puncture wound behind his jaw just beneath his ear. "Stay, Chico. Stay."

The dog didn't move. Ty rushed to the barn and

grabbed the large white metal first aid box, then hurried back.

Through the years, Ty had handled a number of animal injuries and wounds and opted, in this instance, to treat the traumatized Border collie himself rather than drive him to Doc Reynolds's vet clinic in Clayton.

He coaxed Chico away from what remained of Scooter and knelt beside him once again, to treat the major neck wound. "You're a brave dog, Chico. I'm sorry I wasn't here to help you and Scooter."

Ty picked up a pair of scissors from the first aid box and cut the fur from around the two primary puncture wounds left by coyote teeth, then reached for a tube of ointment. "This is going to sting. I'm sorry to have to do it."

He applied the ointment and Chico whimpered and pulled back. "Sorry, boy." He patted him and applied a bandage covering the punctures, confident Chico wouldn't yet be agile enough to scratch it off. "Okay, buddy, now we're going to follow the same steps on that leg gash."

Chico stood patiently while Ty ministered the wound. "You're a good patient, Chico. Good dog." He patted him and stood. "You take it easy now. I'm going to return the first aid kit to the barn and get a shovel. We'll bury Scooter up there under the cottonwood on the side of the hill."

An apricot sun broke over the rolling grasslands as Ty picked up the first aid box and trekked back to the barn.

AT MIDMORNING, Ty and Chico stood over Scooter's grave, covered with fresh soil and large stones. He placed the final stone on the dark earth. "You were a loyal, loving dog, Scooter... Rest in peace, girl."

A few cows and their calves grazed nearby. Hannibal and Trotter stood on the crest of the hill, watching him with three of the other ranch horses.

Ty took in the scene and its almost hallowed serenity. He leaned on the shovel as the prairie grass blew in gentle waves across the land while the sun shone through the branches and leaves of the cottonwood, touching the ground with patterns and colors like a stained glass window.

"This is our cathedral." Ty patted Chico. "If I had been home, boy, you wouldn't have been chewed up by those coyotes—and we wouldn't be burying Scooter..."

His eyes moistened.

CHAPTER 18

Several weeks had passed since their previous visit, when Mother Superior Katherine Hebert invited Sister Sandra Donovan to her office once again. Early evening approached, the end of another rigorous workday.

"Have you given our earlier conversation any thought?" The Reverend Mother sat behind her desk. Her voice had softened since their previous encounter.

Sandra, seated in one of the two chairs on the other side, nodded. "I have, Reverend Mother."

"And?"

"I have examined myself more deeply, as a religious sister and as a person." She looked down at her hands, then back up at Katherine. "I would like to accept your offer to allow me to return home to New Mexico for a week or two. My mother and father will provide funds for my bus fare."

"I am wise enough to realize that such a visit might further challenge your commitment to Christ and to your calling," she sighed, "but, very well, Sandra, you have my permission." She looked at the calendar on her desk and hesitated momentarily. "You may leave week after next. That will give me time to realign staffing."

"Thank you, Reverend Mother."

"You're welcome, Sandra." She paused. "I pray you will ask for God's guidance in resting your mind and your body and that you return safely with a renewed commitment." She pointed to the office window, a tremor in her hand. "Actually, this might be a good time to travel. Before cooler fall weather sets in."

SISTER SANDRA looked down at the brass doorknob as she closed the Reverend Mother's office door, then she walked to the head of the stairway a few feet away and stopped. She wondered why the Reverend Mother's attitude had softened since their previous encounter and what brought about a more congenial presence. Both, she decided, were attributable more to fear of losing another nun rather than any sort of affection toward that nun.

She started down the wooden stairs and thought of home, which she had not visited for several years; the Miami homestead, family and friends, and Ty Daggett. Was Ty still the strapping, muscular cowboy she remembered? Her mother mentioned Ty from time to time in her letters. He was not yet a married family man. Sandra reached the ground floor and exited the building, breathing deeply of the Baton Rouge evening air.

SEVERAL HUNDRED MILES to the west, the sun had just slipped behind the horizon and daylight began to fade when Ty pulled into a parking spot at Clayton Ranch

Market, a popular grocery store on First Street serving the surrounding communities in northeast New Mexico, Texline, Texas, and Oklahoma's panhandle. Chico poked his head out the passenger side window.

"I'll be right back, boy." Ty opened the truck door and stepped down. His dirt-coated, sweaty work clothes showed a hard day's labor. As he made his way toward the store, he noticed Alysa loading two bags of groceries into her car. He smiled and walked over. "Hi there, young lady." He put his arm around her waist. "How's life treating you?"

Alysa turned. "Ty." She closed the car door. "What a pleasant surprise."

"You doing okay?"

"Oh, yes. I'm doing fine, Ty. Just got off work." She brushed her hair back and cast a glimpse at his clothes. Then she grinned. "Looks like you did, too."

Ty shoved his hands in his back pocket. "Busy day, all right. Cleaned the stalls and shoed a couple of the horses."

Alysa reached inside her purse for her car keys.

"We'll have to enjoy dinner together again soon," Ty said. He placed a hand against the small of her back.

Alysa looked aside then back at him. "Ty."

"Yes."

"About the other night."

"Uh-huh." He lowered his hand.

"I need more time."

"What do you mean?"

"I need more time to find myself." She turned aside again. "I'm not sure I want to move here permanently."

"Oh," he said, his eyes widening. "How come? I thought you liked it here."

"I don't think I could live on a ranch out in the middle of nowhere." She bit the side of her cheek. "It just wouldn't work."

Ty furrowed his brow. "Even though you haven't been out there yet, I assume you may be talking about my ranch, Alysa."

She nodded.

"Well," he glanced down at his mud-coated boots, "this turn of events is kinda sudden." He said nothing for a moment. "But I can probably understand. Living on a ranch takes some getting used to."

Alysa held her car keys in one hand. She placed her other hand on Ty's arm. "We'll still see each other from time to time."

"I'm sure we will, Alysa." He tipped his hat and smiled. "I'd best get inside before they run out of stuff." He raised his hands and placed them on her shoulders. Then he leaned forward and kissed her forehead.

CHAPTER 19

The noon hour was drawing to a close in Logan when Gordon opened the door of his apartment after the two-hour return trip from Clayton. With no agenda to follow or takeoff deadline to meet, the journey was more relaxed than the precisely timed nighttime drive.

He stared blindly at the white refrigerator door, mentally composing the letter until, as it did from time to time, his mind drifted elsewhere. Looking around the small apartment, Gordon marveled at its orderliness and cleanliness, particularly the kitchen. He had the Army to thank for that, but Molly would be amazed. He wondered where she was. And what she was doing. He took another swig of beer and returned his attention to the blank page in front of him.

After taking a deep breath, he placed the point of the cheap liquor store ballpoint pen against the tablet. It didn't budge. He relaxed his fingers. The pen began to move across the yellow lined page.

Dear Editor,

My name is Gordon Meese and I just got home from a mission

He stared at the sentence. "Shit!" He tore the page from the tablet, wadded it up in a ball, and tossed it at the white plastic wastebasket beneath the sink. And missed. He looked down at the tablet and tried again.

Dear Sir,

I am a pilot and I just flew a mission. Here's what I did and why.

He examined the feeble statement and shook his head, then ripped the page from the tablet, wadded it, and threw it at the wastebasket. And missed again.

The refrigerator door beckoned. He grabbed another beer, then glanced over at the notepad on the kitchen counter where he'd listed the addresses of twenty-seven newspapers and television stations in New Mexico and Texas. He scanned the list, tossed it back on the counter and returned to the table.

Dear Sir,

I am the pilot of a Cessna aircraft number 5877 and I have just returned home from raising the New Mexico flag

Two hours passed and Gordon looked down and read what he'd written on one of the few remaining pages of the tablet. "I think we've got it this time."

Dear Sir or Madam,

I am the pilot of Cessna 5877 and have just returned from installing the flag of the State of New Mexico at its true and legal position as specified by the United States Congress in 1850 - the 103rd meridian at the 32nd parallel, three miles east of

the position shown on today's maps. Since a sur-
veying error was made in 1859, the State of Texas
has claimed a significant piece of land from its
panhandle south – which rightfully belongs to New
Mexico. This error represents 603,485 acres of New
Mexico land stolen by Texas. A photograph of the
New Mexico flag flying at New Mexico's true south-
east corner is attached. I raised it myself. My busi-
ness card with my cellular telephone number is
attached. I am available for an interview to discuss
with you this violation of New Mexico's eastern
boundary which has persisted far too long.

Yours truly,
Gordon Meese
Logan, New Mexico

Wads of yellow tablet paper surrounded the kitchen wastebasket. Only two of the projectiles had made it inside the basket. He patted the tablet with the final letter, pushed it aside and opened another beer. Then he placed a frozen macaroni and cheese dinner in the microwave oven and turned it on.

The next morning Gordon typed the letter and took it to a friend with a tax and accounting business west of town. They ran off photocopies which Gordon then mailed to newspapers and television stations in Santa Fe, Albuquerque, Clovis, and Hobbs in New Mexico, plus Austin, Dallas, Amarillo, Lubbock, and Midland/Odessa in Texas. Then he drove to Conchas Lake, near Tucumcari, for two days of fishing.

Days passed and he heard from no one. Three weeks

passed, then a month. Not one newspaper or television station called him.

He telephoned Ken Lively. "I sent out twenty-seven goddamn letters to newspapers and television stations and not a goddamn one of them has contacted me."

"You could have saved yourself some postage expense, Sarge. Like I told you, no one gives a rat's ass anymore. This has all been hashed over, talked about, and fought about for 150 years. Let it go!"

"Kenneth, Texas is fucking violating New Mexico's territorial boundary!"

"And nobody gives a shit! Move on to something else," he sighed. "You're supposed to be enjoying retirement, not setting yourself up for a heart attack."

"Like move on to what, for Christ's sake?"

Ken paused. "Like dinosaurs. You're interested in dinosaur tracks."

"Humph."

"Next Friday let's go to Clayton Lake. You look for dinosaur tracks and I'll go fishing. Then we'll come over to my place in Texline and have a fish fry."

"Horseshit!"

"I'm serious!"

"I don't give up that easily."

"I know you don't, Sarge. But you've been chasing this one too long already. And you're close to losing your pilot's license as well. I'll meet you at Clayton Lake Friday morning. 9:00 AM."

THAT SAME DAY Ken and Gordon made plans to meet

at Clayton Lake, an item appeared in a *Fort Worth Star-Telegram* gossip column:

> *One of our reporters came across a letter sent to the Star-Telegram from Gordon Meese of Logan, New Mexico, regarding a New Mexico flag he planted at what he claims is the true position of New Mexico's southeast corner. (Here we go again, people! This "injustice" has been beat to death for 15 decades! Forget about it.) Our same reporter found in a disciplinary file over at FAA's Air Traffic Control Center at 13800 FAA Road, a letter of reprimand for unsafe flying (in the vicinity of Bronco). The letter is addressed to one Gordon Meese of Logan, New Mexico. Might there be a connection? Efforts to contact pilot Gordon Meese have been unsuccessful.*

Two eastern New Mexico newspapers picked up the story from the wire service: *The Quay County Sun* in Tucumcari and the *Union County Leader* in Clayton. Both papers scheduled the story for next-issue publication.

CHAPTER 20

Meanwhile, in Clayton, Ty drove into the parking area at Bradley Hardware & Feed on Front Street. Chico stood on the passenger seat with his head out the window. Ty turned off the engine and patted the dog. "Be right back."

When he entered the store, Henry Lewis and Antonio Cervantes, a neighboring rancher, were leaning over the counter reading the weekly *Union County Leader* newspaper.

"Must be an interesting article," Ty said.

"As a matter of fact, it is." Henry looked up. "As a matter of fact, it is. Look at this, Ty." He placed his finger on a front-page article accompanied by two photographs. "Our buddy, Gordon Meese, is stirring things up. He's, by God, starting a war with Texas!" He laughed.

The caption beneath the first photo read Gordon Meese; the second photo, The New Mexico flag flying at the 103rd meridian and 32nd parallel. Beneath them, an article about Gordon planting the flag in Texas and his subsequent receipt of a flight violation from the FAA.

Ty glanced at the newspaper article and the photos. "Well, I'll be go to hell!" He tipped his Stetson back and grinned.

"Evidently he keeps his airplane here at the airport," Antonio said. "I think I've seen him around. But he lives in Logan where he used to work. Sounds like a real character."

Ty studied Gordon's photograph. "Gordon's a character, all right," he chuckled. "The real thing."

"The guy's a hero," Henry said. "He's waging a one-man battle with the State of Texas for that three-mile strip. More than 600,000 acres. Can you believe it?" He stroked his moustache. "He's a friggin' hero!"

Ty grinned. "I saw Gordon at the Eklund one night a few weeks ago when I was there having dinner. The old boy appeared to be celebrating. I think he'd had one or two hot toddies."

"He had a right to, by God." Henry said. "Hell, we should have a parade for the guy. Right down Main Street. Yes, sir, that's what we oughta do. Right down Main Street!"

"Brass band and all," Antonio chimed in.

"What brings you to the feed store this morning, Ty?" Henry said.

"Picking up a couple of 50-pound salt blocks."

"I need to get one or two myself. How are you and Trotter getting along these days?"

"Trotter's quieted down and yours truly is a little more patient than he used to be." Ty laughed. "We're getting along fine. He's a good horse, Henry."

"I knew he would be."

"I'm going to begin using him more for the hard work and let Hannibal start smelling the roses."

"He deserves every one of 'em. Every single one

of 'em," Henry said.

Ty purchased the salt blocks and carried them out to the pickup. He lifted the blocks to the bed of the truck and closed the tailgate when a car pulled up.

Alysa rolled down the window. "Hello, Ty."

Ty turned. His heart took an extra beat. He had thought about Alysa and their uncomfortable encounter at Clayton Ranch Market the previous week; about her ways being more sophisticated than his own. He was bonded to ranch life and the smell of horses and cattle. In fairness to Alysa, he couldn't ask her to live on the ranch. Nor could he live the city life.

After an awkward moment, he tipped his hat. "You on your way to work?"

"No." She kept both hands on the steering wheel. "I have the day off. Out doing some shopping and I saw your truck." She looked up at him and squinted in the sunlight. "Are you okay?"

"Yeah, I'm fine. How's that cat, Miss Clemmie?"

"She's spoiled as ever. How are Chico and Scooter?"

Ty looked down at his boots then glanced up at the truck cab. "Chico's up there in the cab. A pack of coyotes killed Scooter. I was going to say something when I saw you at the grocery store the other day, but decided not to."

"Oh my God, Ty. I'm so sorry."

"Thanks. She was a good pooch." He glanced at the truck cab. "Chico sure misses her. They were good buddies. I miss her, too."

"When did it happen?"

"The night we were at your place." He put his hands

in his back pockets. "When I got home it was almost daylight… I found Chico pretty beat up and Scooter dead. Chico's still healing. We buried Scooter on a hillside near the corral."

She reached out and touched his arm. "I'm so sorry, Ty. Wish there was something I could do."

"There really isn't, Alysa. But thanks."

"Maybe I can have you over to the house for dinner sometime."

"That's nice of you, Alysa. Very kind of you. But I'm pretty busy at the ranch."

She dropped her hand. "I understand, Ty." She started the engine. "I've been busy at work, too." She glanced up at him. "Be good to yourself."

"I will." He smiled and touched the edge of his hat brim.

She released the brake and the car moved toward the street. Then she stopped and backed up. "I might be moving back to Texas."

Ty placed his hand on the edge of the window. "Oh, really? So soon?"

"I don't like living alone. Did enough of that with Michael." She looked toward the front of the car, then back at Ty. "An old flame back in Bryan phoned me the other night. I'm meeting him in Amarillo this weekend. He'll be there on business."

"I hope it all works out for you."

"Goodbye, Ty."

"Goodbye Alysa."

As she drove off, Henry walked up to Ty. "Was that the nurse from the hospital? The one we saw at the

Rabbit Ear Café?"

"Yeah, that was Alysa Cody."

"Thought I recognized her."

"Some things are meant to be, Henry, and some things aren't. And it is often best to find out sooner instead of later." Ty let the words echo in his mind, but they didn't soften the agonizing edge of hurt. He wondered what it would take to make it go away.

"Yeah, I suppose it is, pardner." Henry patted Ty's shoulder. "I suppose it is."

CHAPTER 21

Gordon and Ken met at Clayton Lake State Park Friday morning as planned. While Gordon examined dinosaur tracks at the northeast side of the lake, Ken stood a half-mile away, casting his line into the clear water from North Point.

AT THE SAME TIME, two disc jockey comedians were getting wound up on their FM morning talk show in Austin, Texas. Rick Cassidy and Randy Livingston, with their live broadcast on "The Rick and Randy Show."

Rick said to Randy, "I just came across an article in the *Fort Worth Star-Telegram* about a guy in New Mexico who claims Texas stole a three-mile strip of land from New Mexico."

"No, Rick, Texas wouldn't do anything like that!"

"It says so right here. I'll read it to you. 'Gordon Meese of Logan, New Mexico planted a New Mexico flag at the true position of New Mexico's southeast corner.'"

"What does Mr. Meese think is the *untrue* position?"

"Where it is now, Randy. Three miles west."

"Well, here we are in Austin, the Capital City of the

Great State of Texas. I think we should telephone the office of The Honorable Jerry Patterson, our Commissioner of the Texas General Land Office, and tell him about this error. Don't you think he should be made aware of such a momentous discovery?"

"I've got a better idea. I telephoned the *Star-Telegram* reporter who wrote the article and he gave me *Mr. Meese's* telephone number! I think we should telephone him first."

"Okay, radio listeners, stand by. You are witnesses to history. We are dialing Mr. Gordon Meese's telephone number right now. Together we are going to hear the story of evil, bad, conniving Texas stealing land from our neighbors to the west."

Rick chimed in. "You will be telling your children and your grandchildren that you were there! You heard Rick and Randy talking to Gordon Meese of Logan, New Mexico!"

"Don't go away, folks!" Randy announced. "You can hear the phone ringing. Soon we will hear the voice of Mr. Gordon Meese himself."

DOWN ON HIS hands and knees, gazing over the edge of the half-mile wooden boardwalk beside Clayton Lake, Gordon studied the deep footprints made by Iguanodontid dinosaurs a hundred-million-years ago. With no other visitors around, he was in deep concentration, captivated by the impressions and visualizing dinosaurs marching up this very path. Hundreds of prints were preserved in the immediate vicinity of this

"Dinosaur Freeway."

Without warning, he was jolted by his cellular telephone ringing in his shirt pocket. He reached for the wooden railing running along the boardwalk, and pulled himself up to a standing position. He stood with one hand on the railing and the other holding the cellphone against his ear. "Hello."

"Is this Mr. Gordon Meese?" an unfamiliar voice said.

"Yes, it is. Who is this?"

"You are talking to the Rick and Randy Show in Austin, Texas, Mr. Meese. I'm Rick."

"And I'm Randy. We're calling you live on our radio show this morning."

"No kidding?" Gordon grinned.

"No kidding. We read about your dispute with the State of Texas over a three-mile strip of land. That's why we're calling you."

Rick piped in. "We understand you flew your own airplane down near the southeast corner of New Mexico to correct the state boundaries and you planted the New Mexico flag in Texas!"

"That's right," Gordon said. "I'm glad you heard about it. This is really exciting to be visiting with both of you."

"That wasn't a very nice thing to do, Mr. Meese."

"Excuse me!"

"Rick and I are Texans. Proud Texans. We and our radio listeners want to know why you would pull a stunt like this."

Gordon growled. "Are you wise guys making light of this?"

"Why, no, Mr. Meese," Rick said. "We just want to

know what gives you the right to fly into Texas and declare the state boundaries are in error."

Gordon felt his face turn red hot. He tightened his grip on the phone. "Listen here, you two assholes—"

After a bleep on the radio transmission, the line went dead.

Randy jumped in. "Folks, we apologize for that language you just heard. Our seven-second tape delay obviously malfunctioned."

"This is Rick, and I join Randy in his apology. You just never know when things like this might happen. We'll break now for a traffic report."

"…and I don't need to put up with this shit!" Gordon shouted. "Do you hear me? Goddamn you!"

No one answered.

"You arrogant bastards!" He flipped the cell phone cover closed and shoved it back in his shirt pocket.

Still holding on to the wooden railing, he steadied himself. "Shit-eating smartasses." His gaze dropped to the dinosaur tracks just inches beneath his feet, leading away from the shore of the lake, parallel tracks heading north.

He got down and set his back against one of the support posts, then wrapped his arms around his legs. He rested his head on his knees and after several minutes looked up and imagined majestic dinosaurs lumbering northward along the Interior Seaway coastline and the Laramidia land mass while, a short distance away, underwater currents were preparing the terrain of present day plains, prairies, and farmlands.

He pictured the spot 300 miles southeast of

Clayton Lake, where the water level became shallow and ultimately disappeared as the Rocky Mountains rose, and where he erected the flag of New Mexico.

Gordon yearned for his cave and his friends, the bats. He didn't bother the bats and the bats didn't bother him.

He reached to the guardrail and pulled himself up. Then he turned toward the spillway path beside the lake and walked around it to the parking lot and the Jeep.

Trees around the lake, their leaves beginning to show hints of yellow and rust, announced the arrival of fall. He paused at a viewer's bench overlooking the water and sat watching the water as it splashed against the rocky shore. He stared without really seeing it.

The answer came to him slowly. He was nothing more than a grain of sand on the infinite beach of time. In the grand scheme of things in the Universe and on Planet Earth, his obsession with the three-mile strip may have become a senseless waste of time and energy.

"Why should I give a tinker's damn about the boundary between New Mexico and Texas? Would the dinosaurs care?"

Gordon rose from the bench and stood for a few minutes. He rubbed his hand across the two-day growth of beard on his face. "Those two boneheads. They can kiss my ass!"

He reached to the ground and picked up a flat stone, then wound up and sent it skipping across the surface of the lake.

With a spring in his step, Gordon turned and continued around the lake perimeter to the parking lot a mile away. Maybe Ken had caught some fish for dinner.

IN SOUTHWEST KENTUCKY, *The Fort Campbell Courier* newspaper had also picked up the story of Gordon Meese from the wire service. A headline on the second page read: "Texas Steals Land from New Mexico!"

Molly Riordan, newly appointed principal of the elementary school north of Oak Grove, sat at her desk. She and her husband, Billy Riordan, a quarter horse rancher, had been married following her third year teaching school.

Molly took a few moments to unwind at her desk at the end of a busy workday and a just concluded Parent-Teacher meeting. She sipped from a glass of ice water and began reading the article about the land steal. Her eyes widened, she broke into a grin, then erupted in laughter. "Gordon Meese, you devil! You sly devil! I am so damned proud of you!"

CHAPTER 22

Ty sensed the wane of fall and subtle signs of winter as he and Trotter, with Chico not far away, worked the roundup of the Black Angus herd in the large summer pasture in the second week of October. Antonio Cervantes rode over with his dog, Jake, to help drive the herd to their winter pasture. Ty and Chico would return the favor driving Antonio's cattle the following week.

The summer pastures, on flat rolling grasslands, afforded little protection and were at a greater distance from the ranch house and barn than the winter pasture. The winter grounds contained more trees and gullies to shield the herd from cold northern winds and heavy storms.

Grazing with the herd of Angus were a white-faced Hereford mama cow and her calf that Ty had bought a month earlier at the Wednesday auction in Clayton. They were brought into the show arena to be sold together or separately. He purchased both of them on impulse, not wanting to see the two separated.

Ty and Antonio, with Chico and Jake, completed the drive and the cattle were settled on their winter grounds by late afternoon. They grazed near creek bottoms beneath the tan and rust-colored bluffs. With the

Hereford mother cow grazing at the far side of the herd, Ty figured the calf must be close by. He and Antonio shook hands and Antonio headed back across open country to his ranch with Jake right behind him.

Ty, aboard Trotter, turned toward home. Chico ran beside them. A few snowflakes fluttered in the air as he reached forward and patted Trotter on the neck. "I think we got the herd to safe ground just in time, boy."

A strong cold front was moving down the eastern slopes of the Rocky Mountains toward northeast New Mexico and the Oklahoma/Texas panhandles. To the north, the sky had turned cast-iron black. The temperature dropped several degrees each minute.

Ty looked down at Chico trotting beside them. "You did a good job today, Chico. I've got a tasty bone waiting for you back home."

Snowflakes increased in number and visibility worsened. Though Ty couldn't see it, he knew, from the weather forecast, that the jet stream was advancing steadily southward and would soon collide with warm, moist air from the Gulf of Mexico. Classic components of an early winter storm. The temperature continued to drop and visibility decreased to a quarter of a mile. The ranch house was about two miles ahead, somewhere beneath the ominous sky.

Ty pulled his weatherworn Stetson down over his eyes and patted Trotter. "I'm proud of you, Trotter. You've graduated, boy." He looked down at Chico. "We're almost home, buddy."

Snowfall became heavier as they crossed a gully with scattered rocks and boulders at its center and shallow cliffs on either side. Suddenly came the bawl of a calf. A piteous, agonizing bawl.

Ty stopped Trotter and listened. He heard it again, coming from behind them. He turned Trotter around and called to Chico. "Chico! Go find him, boy!" The dog took off running toward the sound of the calf. Ty kept Trotter at a walk for fear he'd trip over one of the snow-covered rocks.

Chico barked and Ty turned Trotter in his direction. As they got closer, he squinted until he spotted the dog standing beside the injured brown-and-white Hereford calf. Chico panted and wagged his tail. His eyes had narrowed to slits in the snowy crosswind.

Ty remembered seeing the mother cow in the winter pasture so she was safe. Most mama cows are inseparable from their calves. From time to time, though, he would find a cow like the Hereford, who, apparently, just forgot about her calf and moved on with the herd.

He got down from the saddle and walked to the calf. His left rear leg was trapped in the crack of a narrow crevice in the gully bed. He knelt and examined the animal. The leg wasn't broken, but it was badly bruised from his frantic efforts to free himself. The exhausted calf hadn't yet fully grown its winter coat. With his thinner coat, he wouldn't survive a night of freezing wind and snow.

Ty patted Chico, then walked to Trotter and removed a coil of rope tied to the side of the saddle. He knelt beside the calf and tied one end of the rope around his neck. "I'm going to free that leg, young fella. And when I do, I don't want you to take off looking for mama."

He tied the free end of the rope around his waist, then reached down into the crevice, grasping the calf's leg and working it around the lip in the fissure that had trapped it.

The calf stood, its strength nearly spent, with no sign of wanting to escape. Almost dark, the wind reached down from the north, becoming stronger. Snowflakes settled, only to be whirled away once again.

The calf was too large for Ty to carry it in the saddle as he had done with smaller injured calves in the past. And he knew the danger of leaving the rope tied to his waist only to find himself being dragged across the rock-strewn countryside, should the calf find renewed energy and decide to bolt. He removed the rope and held it in his hand.

Then he reached down and scratched Chico's ears. "Let's walk home, Chico." He took Trotter's reins and tied the right rein around the saddle horn, holding the left rein in his other hand.

As they worked their way up the side of the gully and crested the top, Ty looked ahead to where, on a clear night, he'd be able to see the house and barn in the distance. He saw nothing. Only the dark of night and a blinding snow. Stinging needles of snow hit his face. He placed his gloved hand on the horse's rear end. "Trotter, I'm going to depend on your homing instinct—and Chico's—instead of my own. Lead the way, boy." He patted Trotter's rump and the young horse moved out.

The snow wasn't deep, but the northern wind was relentless. Ty, trudging forward in darkness and cold, was concerned about Chico at his side and the calf behind him, but didn't want to delay their forward progress for a health check. Trotter held fast in pressing toward home.

They had been moving at a slow, steady pace for nearly an hour when Trotter suddenly stopped. Ty walked forward. "What is it, boy?" With his numb hand, he reached up to pat Trotter's muzzle when his elbow bumped against something. He turned. It was the metal gate to the pasture behind the barn and corral. "Well, I'll be damned."

Hannibal nickered from the other side of the gate to welcome them home.

Few times in his life had Ty shown emotion. This was one of those times. "Thanks Trotter. You saved us, boy…" He patted the horse's cheek. "You saved us."

TY BROUGHT Trotter and Hannibal and two other horses from the pasture beside the corral into the barn. He fed and watered them along with the calf. While the calf was taking care of his hunger, Ty knelt on the dirt floor of the barn and treated his wounded leg. Then he stood and stretched. He reached down and patted Chico and the two of them walked toward the barn door and the ranch house 25 yards away. Before he stepped outside into the blowing snow, he turned to see Trotter leaning down to nuzzle the calf with a gentle snort.

A pickup Ty didn't recognize in the dark was parked in front of the house. As he and Chico approached the truck, the driver started the engine and turned on the headlights. He walked to the truck and crossed in front of the headlights to the driver's side.

The driver turned off the engine and stepped out. "I was hoping I'd get to see you, Ty," the woman said.

The woman's voice sounded familiar.

Ty stopped. He and the woman faced each other, separated by only a few feet. Ty's Stetson was seated firmly on his head and pulled down in front to protect his eyes from the snow.

The woman, wearing a heavy winter coat, was bareheaded. Snow accumulated on her hair and eyelashes. She stood with her hands in the large pockets of her sheepskin coat, her eyes a squint.

Chico stood at Ty's side, his tail moving from side to side in welcome to their new guest.

"Sandra?" Ty asked. "Sandra Donovan?"

Snowflakes bounced off Sandra's pale eyelashes. "Hi, cowboy," she said with a smile.

Ty reached out and, as he wrapped his arms around Sandra, he realized the love he had felt for her—his FFA partner, the girl from Miami—had never gone away. Perhaps it had been puppy love. It was love nonetheless.

"My God, it is good to see you," he whispered. He held her for several moments, then stepped back as snowflakes danced and swirled around both of them. "You look wonderful!"

Sandra studied the cowboy standing in front of her and shook her head almost imperceptibly. Her eyes teared. "So do you, Ty."

Ty caught himself. He stepped back. "I'm sorry, Sandra. I apologize."

"Apologize for what?" She turned her head.

"I'm forgetting you're a nun."

Sandra poked the end of Ty's nose with her index finger. "Don't you even think of apologizing, Ty Daggett." She smiled. "I'm loving every moment of it."

Ty grinned. "Let's go inside." He reached for her arm while Chico stood at their side still wagging his tail.

"Just a second. Mom baked two apple pies this afternoon and we both remembered how you love apple pie." She opened the truck door and reached across the truck seat. "So I brought one over for you." She handed it to him. "Good thing you showed up because I was just about to take it back home."

Strands of gray streaked through her Irish red hair, and a couple of wrinkles showed that weren't there when they last saw each other. Ty had aged as well and, despite the just harrowing walk through a blizzard, his energy had been restored.

"You are a fantastic sight for these tired, wind-burned eyes." He handed the apple pie back to her. "You carry this. I'm likely to drop it."

CHAPTER 23

Ty opened the front door of the house and took Sandra's hand. They went inside and he stopped. "Wait here."

He walked around the living room and kitchen, turning on lights while Sandra stood and grasped cherished memories of teenage years, when the two of them had worked on Future Farmers of America projects in this very space.

Ty took her hand again and led her to the kitchen table. "Have a seat while I get a steak bone from the fridge for Chico."

While Chico stretched out on his throw rug and held the T-bone between his paws and gnawed, Ty stoked the wood stove and did a quick glance around the kitchen. The windows needed washing as did the curtains, but all in all, the place appeared to be in pretty fair shape for a woman guest. He washed his hands at the kitchen sink and joined Sandra at the table.

"SO I BEGAN to question—to seriously question—my commitment to the Church." Sandra wasted no time. She unloaded on Ty, as though the words had been trapped inside her, awaiting his presence; words demanding to be released, as if this was a discussion continuing from yesterday.

"Today's Church. How can I explain it? So much has changed, Ty, since I left home to become a novice. And there is so much that refuses to change. Like the Vatican and our omnipotent American bishops who consistently discount women of the Church."

Ty raised his eyebrows. "Whoa. Slow down, girl." They were seated across from each other. "That kind of talk can get you thrown out, can't it?"

"Years ago, probably. Today it would be unlikely. There are fewer nuns and religious sisters every day. If I were to be thrown out, there might not be another sister to take my place."

"I have a hunch there's more to the story."

Sandra sat looking down at her clasped hands. Then her eyes rose and met his. "There is more."

He sat back and folded his arms. "Let it all out, kiddo."

"I can't carry on like this with anyone else, Ty. It has been so long since we were together, the two of us talking about anything and everything."

"I know. We always shared a lot with each other. Which I've missed." Ty smiled. "But, you need to get this out. Go on."

Sandra clasped her hands to her lips and returned his smile. "A nun or a religious sister questioning those in authority certainly isn't encouraged. And rigid rules and traditions are necessary in the religious world, as they are in your lay world. But too often, common sense isn't allowed to override rigidity. Priests and popes call the shots. Women have little say."

Her head fell back and she laughed. "Would you listen to me? Good heavens, if my mom and dad could hear this, they'd have a tizzy fit. An honest-to-God tizzy fit!"

"Don't be so sure of that," Ty cautioned. "My bet is that they'd understand. Would you like a glass of wine?"

"That would be nice. Thank you." She was dressed in jeans, a plaid flannel shirt, and work shoes. She glanced at Chico, on the throw rug near the back door, working on the steak bone. "I like Chico."

"Chico has been a good dog. Someone at a truck stop abandoned him a few years back. Doc Reynolds, our local vet, gave him to me. Don't know what I'd do without him."

"Is he your only dog?"

"I had another dog named Scooter. She and Chico were inseparable. A pack of coyotes killed her a while back."

"How sad—for both you and Chico." Her face softened. "One of my parents' dogs had a litter a few weeks ago. Would you like one of the pups? Two are left, a male and a female."

Ty handed her a glass of cabernet. "Really? Are they ranch dogs?"

"Of course, they're ranch dogs, Ty Daggett!" She tapped her wine glass against his. "Descendants of Miami's finest!"

"Do you think your parents would let me have one?"

"They'd love it. Would you like the male or the female?"

"I'd prefer the female for her temperament. Two male dogs would be inclined to roam. They aren't always a good influence on each other. And I'd have her fixed."

Sandra emptied her glass. "I'll see what I can do."

"More wine?"

"No, thank you." She smiled. "One glass is plenty."

"Let's get back to the nun business and why you're home."

"Well... Let me put it this way. Even though I took my vows of poverty, chastity, and obedience, I sometimes have difficulty with the obedience part."

"Why am I not surprised?"

"As I was saying," she laughed, "in the health field—my field—politicians and insurance companies write the rules for the care of our patients. We and our doctors, the medical professionals, are told to comply." Sandra turned the empty wine glass in her hand. "I was admonished recently and told this is all God's will. To keep my mouth shut!"

"Oh, boy. That's pretty heavy." Ty chortled. "Press on."

"Very well... I've been thinking recently of our communities and villages in northern New Mexico where I might be of help."

"Would your Order transfer you here?"

"Probably not. I've already asked."

"I'd sure like it if they did." He smiled. "So would Chico."

Sandra nodded and grinned. "It would be nice, wouldn't it?"

"I'd love it." He glanced down at his hands on the

table. He turned them over. "But New Mexico isn't exempt from the political and bureaucratic stuff you're seeing in Baton Rouge."

"I know. But it's probably less intense in rural areas."

"Hmmm… maybe. Maybe not. I don't know." Ty glanced at his wristwatch. "Have you had dinner?"

"I'll grab something when I get home."

"The hell you will!" He reached across the table and grabbed her hand. "That's two hours away, Sandra. And it's snowing. Haven't you noticed? Let me whip something up so you're not driving home on an empty stomach."

She winked at him. "We'll do it together."

THEY HAD FINISHED their apple pie desert when Ty said, "How many more days will you be here?" He tried to mask the eagerness in his voice.

"Four more days. I'm going back on Thursday."

"There's someone I want you to meet before you leave. Dr. Jim Grant over at Union County General."

"I'm not here to interview for a job, Ty. I came back to clear my head and try to get a grip on where I go from here. Where can I do the most good? What is God's will for my life? Do I stay with the Order? Or do I move on."

"Serious stuff."

"It is serious." She stared at the floral design on the small china plate.

"A few minutes with Jim would be very helpful for you. He has his fingers on the pulse of northern New Mexico's healthcare. He knows what's going on.

He can help you determine what is best for you. To remain where you are at the Baton Rouge clinic or push the Order for a transfer." Ty said nothing for a few moments as he studied his hands.

Sandra waited in a silence that matched his quiet intensity.

Ty looked up. "Now that you're back, it's become clear to me. I love you, Sandra. Always have." He took a deep breath. "I think you know that. But I want what is best for you. Not what is best for me. Doc Grant can help you. I promise. Do us both a favor and spend a few minutes with him before you go back."

Sandra said nothing for a few moments. Her mouth twitched, as if there were words—and feelings—she wanted to express, but couldn't. She looked at Ty. "Give me his telephone number, cowboy. I'll try to give him a ring in the morning to see if I can drive over for a brief visit."

THE FOLLOWING AFTERNOON Sandra turned off the engine of her dad's 15-year-old pickup, a hardy work truck with several distinctive dents, dings, and rust spots. She opened the door and walked across the Union County General Hospital parking lot to meet with Dr. Jim Grant in his office, located beside the hospital emergency room.

Doc Grant was not a Catholic, but he was a spiritual man; she intuited that quality the moment they met. She sat in a comfortable upholstered chair facing his desk. Their discussion was not an interview. Rather, it became a conversation between two healthcare professionals, one a physician and the other a nurse, each with genuine respect for the other.

As their thirty-minute appointment drew to a close, Doc Grant said, "I believe I'm doing God's work, Sister Sandra, just as you are. My community of cattle ranchers and farmers is perhaps not as varied as your patient community in Louisiana. But they are my extended family. I feel personally attached to every one of them. When I see a patient here in the hospital or in one of the stores or restaurants of Clayton or one of the neighboring towns, it is very gratifying. In many instances I see the faces of second and third generations."

He picked up a Lucite paperweight on his desk and set it back down. "I suspect you find the same to be true with your patients in Baton Rouge."

"I do. At times, I find myself recalling certain patients. Their faces. Their smiles. Their voices. Sometimes their loneliness."

"In many ways, the two of us answer the same calling. And we each do the best we can." Doc Grant pushed his chair back and stood. "Perhaps one day we'll work together." He held out his hand. "Please keep in touch."

SANDRA'S ARMS WERE folded across her chest as she walked back to her father's pickup and, though she was deep in thought, she sensed a spark in her eyes. She opened the driver's side door and slid behind the steering wheel, then took a deep breath and started the engine.

She drove out of the parking lot to 4th Avenue and the turnoff to the highway to Miami. The sky was a clear deep blue with only a few isolated clouds. Patches of snow remained from the previous day's snowfall; most had melted into the ground. Between Clayton and Springer she saw familiar herds of Black Angus and Herefords and a couple of smaller herds of Holsteins and Guernsey.

As she left Springer on County Road 21 to Miami, 12 miles west, a large raven perched on a wooden fence post, its head rotating from side-to-side, surveying the surrounding territory. One of the most beautiful ravens she'd ever seen, its feathers were a shining luminescent black. She was tempted to stay and study the bird, but opted to continue driving.

On either side of the road stretched rolling grasslands and occasional ranch and farm buildings. Straight ahead, due west, she glanced at the Sangre de Cristo mountain range, brush-painted in hazy shades of gray/purple/blue.

She drove by two herds of antelope before entering a wide left turn where the ranches and homes of Miami came into view at the base of the familiar plateau. The Donovan home, a white two-story frame with dark blue trim, stood out from the rest.

No traffic passed as she pulled off the road and stopped beneath a large cottonwood. She turned off the engine and rolled down the window, then retrieved her rosary from a shirt pocket and began to recite Hail Marys.

Then she stopped, acknowledging the rote recitation, devoid of sincerity or feeling. Only words.

She returned the rosary to the shirt pocket. "Please, God, I need your guidance. My compass is spinning. It needs to stop and point somewhere. You know what I mean? Help me find my bearings. I want to continue serving you and those in need of my help. I must. The world has changed since I left home and travelled down this road to take my vows. The world has changed and I have changed. I'm at a crossroads and I need to choose to remain Sister Sandra Donovan or to remove my veil. Years ago I committed myself, as a nun, to Christ. May I continue that commitment as a lay person? Please guide me. Help me to make the right choice. To honor your will."

She looked to her left. Three farm horses, two blacks and a gray, huddled together in the large pasture on the other side of the road. A scene she had remembered so many times, and recalled from so many places and assorted clinics. This scene of home.

Sandra stepped from the rusted pickup and walked to the fence. The two black horses, a mare and a stallion, approached her. She reached across the barbed wire and patted both of them

"Are the two of you messengers from God?" she said, smiling.

The stallion lifted his head and snorted.

Sandra searched the gorgeous dark eyes of the mare. "What would you do?"

The mare nickered and Sandra laughed. Both horses lowered their heads and began grazing.

"God," Sandra whispered, "I have returned home to find a man who still loves me."

A meadowlark called in the distance.

"And I love him." She clasped her hands together and held them against her chest. "I think you know that."

Another meadowlark answered.

CHAPTER 24

Tuesday night. Earlier that day, Sandra had told Ty she planned to return to the convent and Baton Rouge on Thursday.

After a spaghetti and meatball dinner, Ty sat at his desk in the living room, updating ranch figures on computer spread sheets. It had been a good year with a minimum of livestock lost to illness or injury. There might be money in the bank at the end of the year. One of Johnny Cash's last recordings, "America V," played in the background.

As Ty wrapped up the month's Profit & Loss statement, Chico got up from his throw rug and stood in front of the door. Ty glanced over and watched the Border collie turn his head from side to side, listening to something out on the porch. Someone knocked.

He got up from his chair and walked to the door. Sandra stood on the porch with a ball of fur in her arms, a scruffy puppy with button nose and inquisitive eyes pointed right at him. She set the pup down and it darted across the threshold to Chico. The two dogs engaged in a tail wagging, sniffing contest.

Ty reached for Sandra's arm. "Come on in out of the cold." He gave her a hug and looked down at the pup.

"Look at that raggedy little pooch, would you!"

"Your present from Mom and Dad."

"Wow." He got down on the floor with the two dogs while Sandra looked on. Chico licked his face. The pup followed suit.

"What a sight this is," she laughed. "Wish I had a camera."

Ty endured a few more dog licks, then stood. "Chico will take that little girl under his wing right away." He rested his hands on Sandra's shoulders. "Please thank your folks."

"I will."

"I remember the St. Bernard you had when we were kids."

"Tobias? My dear Tobias?" Sandra said. The two dogs tumbled at their feet.

"Yeah. He was a good dog. I'm going to name the pup Toby."

Sandra looked up and placed her hand on Ty's cheek. "I've missed you."

Ty reached down and took her hand and kissed it. "I love you, kiddo."

When he glimpsed back at Sandra's face, tears glistened in her eyes.

"Ty," she took a tissue from her pocket and wiped her eyes, "instead of me thanking Mom and Dad for giving you Toby…" She wiped her eyes again. "Excuse me…" She blew her nose.

Ty suppressed a grin while, behind him, in their own world, the two dogs tumbled and wrestled in the living room.

"Could you…" Sandra swallowed, "come over to the ranch tomorrow and have dinner with us?"

"I'd love to."

"I've got some things I need to talk about with Mom and Dad." She reached for Ty's hand. "I want you to be there."

CHAPTER 25

At the Donovan Ranch in Miami, during dinner, Sandra announced to her mother and father, and to Ty, her decision to leave the Order and return home.

Sandra's father, Red Donovan, readily accepted her choice.

Her mother did so with hesitation. "I love the thought of your coming home, sweetheart, but I am afraid of any consequences or retribution. Will God and The Church forgive you?"

Ty was more an observer than a participant during the dinner table discussion. But there was no doubt—no doubt at all—how he felt about Sandra's decision. After dinner, when he excused himself and rose to return home, he walked around the table and hugged Sandra. "Can I drive you to the bus station in the morning?"

"I would love that, Ty."

He said good-bye to Sandra's mom and dad and turned toward the door.

"Ty," Red Donovan said, "wait." He got up from the table and walked to Ty. He put his arm around his shoulder. "I'm glad you were here this evening, son. You have always been a member of our family. One of our own." He patted Ty. "Thank you."

"I am honored to have been here, Red." Ty held his Stetson in his hand. "This has been a tough decision for Sandra. She needs our support."

"I do as well, son."

TY AND SANDRA stayed in touch with telephone visits and letters until the April morning when one of Henry's ranch hands arrived at the Daggett ranch to take care of things while Ty drove to Louisiana. The first day, he drove to Dallas; the second day from Dallas to Shreveport to Baton Rouge. At five o'clock that second morning, Ty drove out of a motel parking lot on the outskirts of the Baton Rouge where he'd spent the night following the nine-hundred mile drive. Johnny Cash CDs accompanied him during most of the journey.

Shortly after leaving the motel, Ty stopped at a diner for a light breakfast and cup of coffee. Then he got back in the truck and drove five more miles to the convent. He glanced at his watch. He was right on schedule and he wasn't nervous, as he thought he might be. He was at peace. Freeing, long-awaited peace.

FEW PEOPLE KNEW Sister Sandra Donovan would be leaving. They had attended no farewell dinner the night before. Said no good-byes.

Sandra sat by herself in a small room beside the convent kitchen. Orange juice, toast, and coffee had been placed on the wooden table. No one was there to kiss her or wish her bon voyage and say, "It's been wonderful." It was as though no one wanted to disturb the balance of things.

She ate alone and in silence, looking forward to the future but, at the same time, feeling a sense of failure. "The customary Catholic guilt," Red Donovan would say. In two weeks, she would assume her new position as head of an indigent care facility at Clayton Hospital, under the direction of Doc Grant.

Sandra looked around the room, searching for something familiar or another person. Her hair fell just below her shoulders. A crucifix, the size of her hand, was the only thing on the white wall facing her. Her navy blue veil lay on the table.

She finished her breakfast and walked to the door, then reached for the stainless steel doorknob. Her gut told her she had made the correct decision. Sandra couldn't have written it out, giving logical, convincing reasons. Oh, maybe she could, but why? The time had come.

The time had come to proceed with her life. Continuing to serve God and those in need of her care. As a lay person.

She turned the doorknob and reached down for her small suitcase, then opened the door and walked out, leaving the Order. The door closed by itself.

Baton Rouge had begun to stir. In the early morning light, she walked down the cobblestone pathway toward the pickup waiting by the curb, its engine running.

BEHIND HER, from a second floor office window of the convent, Reverend Mother Katherine Hebert looked down with clasped hands. "May God bless you and care for you, Sandra Donovan."

She turned and sat down at her desk, and didn't move until the convent tower clock chimed six.

TY GOT OUT of the truck and walked around to the passenger side. He took Sandra's suitcase and opened the passenger door. "Let's go home, Sandra."

Sandra reached up and touched his cheek.

CHAPTER 26

Earlier in the morning, in Texline, Texas, Ken Lively rolled over in bed and picked up his ringing cell phone on the nightstand. The room was pitch black.

"Kenneth, my boy, this is Gordon. I'm sitting here studying the Texas/New Mexico border."

"Sarge, it's the middle of the night. I was sound asleep." Ken closed his eyes, hoping this was only a dream. "Can we talk about this tomorrow?"

"No," Gordon said, "hear me out. Those two radio smartasses, Rick and Randy, pissed me off."

Ken yawned. "Let's put this off 'til morning."

"I'm looking at this 1906 letter from the Department of The Interior. The one I found in the state archives. Where they say only Congress can correct the boundary discrepancy."

Ken took another deep yawn. "So, what about it?"

"Kenneth, my boy, I'm going to fucking sue Congress!"

"For Christ's sake, Sarge," Ken squinted at the bedside clock, "it's two-thirty in the goddamn morning!"

TOM CLAFFEY

Tom Claffey spent his growing-up years in northern New Mexico and southern Colorado. He majored in English literature at New Mexico Military Institute and Creighton University and, in 1954, accepted an appointment to West Point. He graduated in 1958 and became a pilot in the U.S. Air Force. In civilian life he worked in investment securities and banking and began writing for publication in 1981. He lives in Santa Fe.